Brave Women

a novel
by

Madeleine Belden

Rouleau Press

ACKNOWLEDGEMENTS

Thanks to Renée Albert for proofreading and to Bill Trotter, whose
skills with the Macintosh were invaluable in getting this done.
Thanks to Chris Young at Hignell, who has the patience of a saint.
I especially wish to thank my husband, Mark, who served as edi-
tor, grammar checker, spell-checker, assistant cover designer and
typesetter for this book, and who always inspired me.

ISBN #0-9656235-2-1

Printed in Canada by Hignell Printing Limited.

Cover Art by Bill Trotter

Photo by Robert Kim

For Marion

one

Diane Turner was a woman in search of the perfect moisturizer. All together she had tried eighty-seven different facial creams, but so far none held true to the promise on the label. The promise that said *use our product and your face will look younger and your life will get better.* It never turned out that way. Even so, Diane continued, religiously trying every fancy facial lubricant out there, secretly hoping that she would one day stumble upon the night cream that would allow her to wake up with Michelle Pfeiffer's face and Gloria Steinem's attitude.

Every year that passed brought more anxiety than the last, and she had no idea why. Diane could only guess at reasons. Unfortunately, none of her stabs at self-diagnosis ever led to any life-altering insights, forcing her to continue housing and feeding her free-floating anxieties. Even when she was in therapy, in her late twenties, it didn't have the kind of effect on her that she had hoped it would. It did not relieve her of the unaccounted-for fear that had always been with her.

Other things did bring relief, however. Knowing that she was bright and highly educated helped. A level of autonomy in her career brought with it a small amount of peace of mind. Lusty looks from married men also provided a degree of serenity. Diane knew that the last of these was not the smartest choice in the world, but hell, it beat Prozac. She did not believe in ingesting chemicals to mask feelings. She did believe in facing emotions head-on. It was the reason that she became a therapist: to one day understand why she herself was so conflicted, and to receive a paycheck at the same time. Now, fourteen years later, she seemed to be no better off.

When Diane was still a Girl Scout she prayed every day for large breasts and a long waist—and later received both. Soon that wasn't enough, and a lifetime of constant comparisons to other females was born. She wanted to be blonde, very blonde. She was certain that that would make her feel different inside, make her feel beautiful. And when she became blonde she did feel different, for a while. Then it was her nose. Diane got a nose job the summer she turned sixteen and paid for it with baby-sitting money. And, as usual, she felt better for a while, until she noticed her teeth needed whitening...

At thirty-eight, she was still a stunning woman. She wore her paid-for blonde hair in a sexy bob parted on the side. When she wanted to be noticed, or perhaps get a cheaper estimate from a mechanic, she let her head fall to the side so that her silken strands cascaded over her green-tinted-contact-lensed right eye. The overall effect was heart-stopping, though the gesture never once brought on a cheaper estimate from a mechanic.

Diane was currently the head of Brave Women, a therapy group that she had started, free of charge to any female. Its purpose was to offer support, understanding and acceptance to any person born without a penis. It was her own way of "giving back." Also, she found Sunday nights inexplicably depressing, and filling the time with these meetings helped. Diane held the gatherings right in her own office that she used for her private practice Monday through Friday. The idea came to her when a referral client, a claustrophobic, kept exclaiming how extremely large and roomy, and non-threatening her office was. Diane realized then that it *was* unusually large, large enough for a meeting.

After the claustrophobic left, Diane looked around the airy, loft-like space. The walls were plain because she didn't want to risk setting off any unstable minds with her taste in art. Pipes and beams were exposed. The wood floors were worn and bore the unmistakable markings of spilled acid, a legacy of the hide-tanning operation that formerly occupied the structure. Diane found it charming. "I could have meetings right here…"

That was a year and a half ago. A lot had happened since then. In fact, recently two members of Brave Women had announced that they had fallen in love—with each other. No one knew what to say, including Diane. The whole group just looked at the two lovers, Kyle and Judy. "I can certainly see why they're attracted to each other—they're both pretty," thought Diane.

It was true enough. Judy was condensed and even-figured, her brunette hair combed into a bow that always seemed to match whatever she was wearing. She loved things neat and orderly, including, especially, her appearance. She wore eyeglasses that appeared to cover her entire face, barely held up by a tiny nose that no one could see. Judy had a joyous, breathy quality, often nodding enthusiastically as she spoke, as if addressing a room full of kindergartners.

Kyle was the same age as Judy, thirty-six, and had the most stunning set of cheekbones that Diane had ever sworn she'd kill for.

"You'll have beautiful children," Diane said, setting off a round of nervous laughter.

Kyle *was* attractive. It made her life easier, and she knew it. It was something that was there, that she didn't have to think about or work at. It seemed, at times, the one thing in her life that wasn't complicated. Once, a man in a bar told Kyle that he could see all the beauty of the desert in her: reddish-brown hair the color of clay, eyes light green like a cactus, and golden complexion like the first rays of the morning sun.

"What do you do for a living," she asked him, "write Hallmark cards?"

"Hardly," he replied. "I sell beautiful paintings done on black velvet."

It was now seven o'clock Sunday night and a lot of bitter females were due in Diane's drafty office for another meeting. The women started filing in and Diane welcomed each one with her usual "I know how awful you feel" smile.

When all the members were seated, their chairs arranged in the shape of a giant W, Diane looked around the room, mentally pairing off women, wondering if another two would hit it off.

"Kyle and Judy won't be here tonight," announced Diane, "they're at Ward's picking out a sofa. So," she continued, "Let's get started. Those of you who are new tonight, welcome. We ask that everything in this room remain confidential and that you cry at least once during the meeting. Who'd like to start?"

A woman in a dark wig and sunglasses, known only as "Carla" stood up.

"I'd just like to say that this is my third meeting, and even though I can't tell you my name, where I work, or where I live, it's so nice to be able to come to a place and be accepted for who I am."

Applause.

"That's why we're here," Diane said, "to love and embrace each other unconditionally, and to help each other become Brave Women. Who'd like to cry now?"

A small, sniffling woman stood up. She scanned the W, and then slowly, pitifully plodded her way from one end of the letter to the other, weeping helplessly to each individual. Then, after every woman had been carefully sobbed to, she let loose one last heaving shudder and collapsed in her seat.

"Next?" asked Diane.

"I'd like to be next," said a voice the group didn't recognize.

The whole W eyed the new member. She was pretty.

"She'll go fast," thought Diane.

"Well, I-I'm new" she fumbled faintly. "My name is Missy, and I came here because..." Missy stopped.

The whole W leaned toward her.

Missy stood before them, hopelessly awkward, her hazel eyes looking down at her size six shoes. Everything about Missy was slight: her height, her weight, her attitude. Her hair was in between shades—neither blonde nor brunette. Her driver's license stated HAIR COLOR: DARK BLONDE/LIGHT BROWN. Missy still bitterly remembered how, in high-school, all the girls had belonged to either the blonde clique or the brunette clique. "Who are *my* people?" she would wonder.

Missy continued. "I guess I-I really came here because I don't know who I am."

"We'll tell you!" shouted someone.

Missy stopped. In her nervousness, she had misstated her purpose. She tried again. "I had heard such wonderful things about you people…"

"We're not people, we're women!" said the one known as Carla.

"Please, let's let Missy speak," said Diane.

The W settled down. Missy's eyes grew wide.

"Well," she said, "the problem is my mother-in-law."

"It usually is," said Diane, shaking her head.

The W turned on Diane. "Let her talk!" they chorused.

"Sorry," Diane said, "Go ahead, please."

Finally there was quiet, and the floor was returned to Missy, which all but overwhelmed her. She could feel them studying her, wondering about her, guessing at how inept a person she was. Suddenly Missy's thoughts were interrupted by someone clearing her throat. Startled, Missy remembered her purpose, and reluctantly focused on the faces in front of her. A wave of inadequacy engulfed her. She discarded it, used to it now after thirty-two years. Missy realized that she was going to have to force herself to tell these ladies the real reason she came here tonight. And they would listen. Why wouldn't they? After all, her problems were just as good as anyone else's. Weren't they? Missy closed her eyes so she no longer had to endure those faces watching her. "Well, my mother-in-law, Estelle, recently started living with us."

There was a small, collective gasp in the room. Missy opened her eyes. Were they agreeing with her? Did they see her point already? For the first time tonight she was almost glad she came. Missy trekked on, cautiously, eyes open. "See, my father-in-law just retired to Texas and she didn't want to go with him. The thing is, now she's living with us and she's...she's...taking over our lives!" She halted, stunned by her own outburst. Missy hesitated, fearful all her life of being the carrier of controversy, and yet imbued with an insistent need to warn the world of her mother-in-law. Missy concentrated on the bare wall behind the women, and forced herself to hurry, worried that these ladies would soon grow impatient with her. "My own personal theory is that she doesn't want to move on to that phase of her life— retirement. It's like...like she wants to live our lives—like she's trying to just suck the youth right out of us."

"She sounds wonderful!"

"Yeah, bring her next time."

Diane stepped in, smiling kindly at a stunned Missy. "Our door is always open—any woman who longs for unconditional love is welcome here, provided we approve of her life choices. And I think I speak for the group when I say we'd all love to swap insights with Estelle."

The entire W nodded.

Missy drove home that night defeated, deflated. She sighed, for she was used to those feelings as well. The thought of going back to that meeting with Estelle was almost too much to bear. It would be like putting a narcissist in a mirrored room. "I don't know if I can do it, although I did promise. Why do I find it so difficult to say no?"

It was her worst flaw. It proved burdensome, directing her life in certain ways that Missy might not have chosen otherwise. The inability to utter the word "no" was responsible for most of her regrets in life. Buying dresses she didn't need, bad haircuts…her marriage?

Missy thought back to the day that she and her husband, Todd, met on a flight from Denver to Pittsburgh. Much too busy to talk because there were drinks to be served and pre-cooked meals to heat, Todd ran up and down the aisles, catering to cranky passengers as Missy timidly looked on. She sat, crowded in her middle airline seat, entranced by his face. It was dark, intense and brooding as he routinely fluffed pillows; marred with perspiration as he suffered endless demands from whiny passengers.

Missy felt an attraction to this harried steward take hold of her. She watched him carefully. Something about him appeared so capable, so definite, so...*there,* unlike herself, who had always seemed so faint, so sketchily rendered in her own mind. Missy found herself drawn to his certainty, his knowing. It was reassuring to her. His confidence seemed to spill over, generously inviting her to share in it. Just observing him, Missy felt happier, more solid, than she had in years.

Later in the flight, when the attraction seemed mutual, Missy was shocked that he would even notice her, let alone seem to like her. Yet there was no mistaking it, he made it fairly obvious that he reciprocated her interest. He seemed quite taken with her, in fact. Twice, Missy looked up from her magazine and found him smiling at her from the galley. When serving drinks, Todd's gaze penetrated Missy as he handed her a plastic cup of 7-Up, then gallantly insisted that she take the rest of the can.

After the rocky flight Missy was struggling to pick up her suitcase at the baggage claim area. It was heavy, filled with tile she didn't need because she was bullied by a pushy salesman. "Why did I have to browse in a Mexican ceramic tile store?" Suddenly, seemingly out of nowhere, Missy watched as something filled the handle of her suitcase. It was a dark, hairy hand followed by a bulging forearm emerging from a short-sleeved steward uniform. Missy looked up and saw a gripping smile. It was Todd, her intense flight attendant.

They went out that night to a movie. In the middle of the film Todd tapped her on the shoulder. She looked up and saw Todd standing next to her in the aisle, leaning over, his hands clasped in front of him saying, "Can I get you anything? Coffee, tea, popcorn?" Missy shook her head and ten minutes later Todd came back from the concession stand with a soda and asked what he had missed.

They dated for three months. Todd insisted that she marry him. He was absolute in his desire that they wed.

Once again, Missy found his clarity an incredible turn-on. He was so different from any man she had ever known before, at least from the kind of men that usually asked her out. The ones that did, Missy found to be as hesitant and unsure as she was. This only served to strengthen Missy's weak self-image.

She was the only child of quiet, flustered people. As far back as she could remember, Missy's parents, it seemed, had been in a state of fixed, steady embarrassment. Even recalling her childhood on a farm in rural Pennsylvania, she could only picture their faces in various shades of red. They were so sheepish, so soft-spoken, in fact, that Missy didn't have a single memory of them ever fighting with one another. Or with anyone else, for that matter. Once, on her tenth birthday, her reticent parents took Missy out for dinner. She ordered a hamburger and a strawberry malt, which she had been dreaming about for a month. It was crowded in the diner, and the tired waitress brought a chocolate malt instead. Missy stared at the unwanted concoction and began to inform the waitress of the mistake when she suddenly noticed her mother and father's crimson faces. The repentant pair silently begged Missy to just accept what she had gotten, and please, not to make a scene.

It was an intense, silent moment in the noisy diner. The same moment in which Missy first felt without a voice. Ineffective, unimportant. They were her parents, and they were telling her that she didn't matter. Not even on her birthday. Missy did as her parents telepathically told her and didn't rock the boat.

Todd was so opposite. It would never occur to him not to speak his mind. It was his nature, and Missy admired him for it. In fact, in the time that they had been dating, in a small way, she had begun to think of him as her role model.

And, in another way, one that she was only partially aware of, Todd became Missy's voice. It was a temptation that she could not resist, though she was somewhat aware of its dangers. That was one reason that Missy found herself wavering when Todd proposed. Did she really love him or was he just fulfilling a need for her? One that she, ideally, ought to be able to fill for herself. There was also another reason that she hesitated, aside from the fact that that was *her* nature. Despite Todd's sturdy cheeriness, there seemed to be one unattractive adjunct to his personality: a small, barely detectable amount of boxed-in rage. Yes, something seemed so...angry, yet sturdily encased. Still, Missy couldn't seem to say no...

It wasn't until after they eloped that she met Todd's parents, Estelle and Todd Senior. The minute Missy and Todd walked into the all-white ranch home Missy was assaulted by stationary cigarette smoke. Desperate for air, Missy took a full moment to get her bearings. Finally, her eyes adjusted, and she could just about make out Todd's dark features through the blue-gray haze. He smiled, reassuring her. She smiled back, and for a split second imagined that she could feel the smoke against her teeth. Just then, Todd's mother, Estelle, came waltzing out in a shiny blue pantsuit and matching turban, arms extended toward her only son. Missy stood dumbstruck, awed by Estelle's casual hostility. It was remarkable. A true artist, she made it look easy. It appeared to Missy that even the cigarette smoke was reluctant to be around her, scattering quickly in every direction wherever Estelle stepped.

Missy watched her new mother-in-law as she fussed over her son, grateful now for the opportunity to observe her unnoticed. Her face was worn and leathery, probably from too many Florida vacations, and heavily made up. Taking in the ruby red lips and false eyelashes, Missy privately wondered how many layers of pancake and powder there were.

"Todd!" Estelle hugged him hard, ran her hands through his dark hair and whispered in his ear. They both laughed out loud, Estelle cackling wildly. She had a deep, gravelly voice, sculpted by years of non-filtered cigarettes.

Todd turned to his shy bride. "Mom, this is Missy."

Estelle turned her turbaned head toward her daughter-in-law. Slowly, she drank in the newcomer.

Ever since the obstetrician said "It's a boy!" Estelle had been anticipating this moment. The moment that she would meet her son's wife. It wasn't that she didn't want it to come, she did. It was only natural. It was inevitable, for any mother who had raised her son flawlessly, as she had. And now, the time was finally here. She was nervous and hoped it wouldn't show. This was it. The changing of the guard, so to speak. Her son was about to reveal his choice in wives, which of course would reflect back to her, and how fine a job she had done in raising him.

She had often daydreamed about whom he would choose as his eternal mate. Estelle knew he would opt for a girl just like his mother—a continuation, if you will, of herself. This would be his final salute to her, a Thank You for all that she had done for him. In fact, in many ways she had looked forward to this moment. She prided herself on the fact that she was not a covetous, clingy mother. On the contrary, Estelle enjoyed fantasizing about her future daughter-in-law—the open relationship that they would have; how Todd's wife would look up to her, see her as a font of knowledge and wisdom that she could tap into. Yes, Estelle was definitely bursting with delight, and yet nervous at the prospect of someone new. It was going to be a change, an adjustment, which, frankly, was not Estelle's strong suit. But she had had thirty-two years to prepare herself, and just knew it would be all right.

She removed her hands from her son, and placed them over Missy's. Estelle then took Missy's right hand and put it over her heart. "Look," she whispered, "This is how glad I am to meet you. My heart is going crazy! Can you feel it? Of course I've got tachycardia too, maybe that's part of it. But I swear, when my only son, Todd, told us that you were married we were ecstatic!"

Momentarily eased by Estelle's somewhat welcoming words, Missy smiled. Estelle still held Missy's hand over her heart, however. She tried, gently, to take it back, but Estelle wouldn't release it, and stood alarmingly close, staring into Missy's eyes. Missy felt sick, partly because of Estelle's overfamiliarity, partly because she could smell her eyelash glue on top of the cigarette smoke.

"There she is!" exclaimed Todd Senior, coming from the kitchen. He took Missy in his arms and hugged her. The three stood there in the foyer and beamed at Missy.

"Isn't she just delicious?" Estelle cooed. "Well, I hope you're hungry! I made corned beef and cabbage because Todd tells me you're Irish!"

"Yes, I am," confirmed Missy.

Estelle grabbed her new daughter-in-law by the arm and held tight as she led her down the single carpeted step, into the colorless living room, deep into the heart of the second-hand smoke.

Later, Todd got a reservationist's job with the airline so he could stay home with his bride. They rented a small house with two bedrooms on the second floor. The two-story dwelling was a deliberate act of rebellion on Todd's part. "It's not much, but it's something," he told Missy. They filled their home with the most vividly colored furniture they could find. More rebellion—this time on Missy's part. The vibrant floral prints on the sofa and matching love seat did little, however, to deter Todd's parents from coming over every Sunday and expecting dinner, and every Sunday Missy's home became filled with unwanted smoke. She soon found out that Estelle was a three-pack-a-day gal and thought mammograms were the biggest rip-off in the entire medical profession.

Missy watched as Estelle busily puffed away and could only hope.

two

Diane lived alone in the same one bedroom apartment she had rented for the past ten years. It had a glorious view of downtown and track lighting. Once a week, the cleaning lady let herself in and vacuumed the light blue wall-to-wall carpet and polished the antique reproduction dining room set Diane had purchased when she received her Master's degree. Diane kept a crystal vase of silk lilacs in the center of the table and insisted that the cleaning lady assiduously dust all the flowers each week, so that they would always look as real and life-like as possible. And each Monday the cleaning lady was also instructed to apply a brand new Glade air freshener to the dining room wall under the light switch, lilac scented.

When Diane got home Sunday night she was exhausted. She immediately turned up the air conditioning, activated the gas-fired log in the fireplace, and ran a bath. Removing her designer clothes at the end of the night was always tough for Diane, who was constantly monitoring her weight, so much so that she felt it necessary to remove even her contact lenses before stepping onto the talking scale. It was always the same, her weight, one hundred and thirty-eight pounds on the nose, which for her height of five-eight was perfect. Nevertheless, perfect was never a word that came to mind in Diane's daily assessment of her physical self. She regarded herself as a work-in-progress, with no end in sight.

Diane re-lived tonight's meeting as she stepped into the tub. Luxuriating in the warm bubble bath, she thought about the ladies of Brave Women. About how they always looked to her as if she had all the answers, which in a way, she liked, even clung to sometimes when she was depressed. "If they only knew the truth..." Diane was referring to her habit of dating married men. Men that had taken a vow in a church to love and honor...someone else. "If anyone ever knew the real me..."

Diane closed her eyes and saw the Brave Women stoning her with a pile of self-help books. Then she saw the look of betrayal on all their faces, and suddenly she was ashamed. Diane was supposed to be the strong one, the leader. If she was so messed up, how could they ever have hope for themselves?

She laid her head back against the white porcelain tub, careful not to get her hair wet. She was too tired to blow-dry it tonight. Diane stared at the maroon bath tiles around the faucet and soon her mind began its habitual, unconscious search for more things to fill her with angst. Slowly, she began chiding herself that maybe she relied too much on academic accomplishments to brace a faltering self-esteem. "Am I just a woman hiding behind a Master's degree?" Diane wondered. She was planning on getting her doctorate in the next few years and realized that perhaps her motivation was fueled by a low opinion of herself. She wrestled with that possibility, annoyed at its implication. Diane hated uncovering new evidence that seemed to support a confidence problem, even if it was just to herself. Especially to herself. She knew that she had issues, but Diane was always telling Diane that she was getting better, gaining more certitude and self-reliance. Then, every once in a while, a realization would rear its ugly head. The answer, for tonight, she decided, was that she was too tired to care. "What's the difference?" she wondered. "Maybe a low self-image has an up side. Maybe it's a great motivator. Maybe I'll meet somebody in the doctorate program," she thought. "Somebody good-looking and smart, and careful with money. A popular guy with a nice speaking voice. And sing-" She started to say the word *single*, but stopped herself. Diane knew it wouldn't matter, because try as she might she could never bring herself to be attracted to any man that wasn't married. Even if she met her dream man, someone with all the qualities that she just described, she'd still be turned off, and she knew it. Diane liked men that someone else had chosen first. It was...comforting, for some reason. And painful.

Diane shook her head and closed her eyes, she didn't want to cry, not now. She knew that she wanted to get married some day, she just had never been sure how to get around her problem. And time was no help, forever working against her. Diane was continually aware of time, aware of the moments speeding by and then gone forever. "Oh, God, I've got a birthday coming up," she realized. "Thirty-eight years. Wait! I'm going to be thirty-*nine* years old! Thirty-nine and I'm still a married man junkie." Diane blinked, her body unmoving under the soapy water. She sat dormant as something was dawning on her. She had never thought about it like that before. For some reason, at this moment, a behavior she was previously adjusted to now felt wrong, no longer acceptable, no longer thrilling. Why? she wondered, eyes down, staring at the water. Diane thought for a second, then closed her eyes. It was the word "still", she decided. "I'm still just a married-man junkie." She sat, shivering in the warm water.

Diane got out of the tub and went into her bedroom to put on her silk pajamas. She glanced at the picture on her dresser. It was her current married lover's photo; unfortunately, it also included his wife and two children, because that was the only picture he could give Diane. In the photo, taken at an amusement park, they were all wearing Old West costumes. "It's better than nothing," thought Diane, pulling her pajama top over her head.

●

His name was Joe and they met accidentally in the pornographic section of the video store. He spoke to her.

"Can you recommend anything?" he asked.

She did a double take, unsure if she had heard him right. He repeated the question, and in fact seemed to revel in her obvious discomfort. "I'm in here by mistake—I'm looking for a comedy," she said.

"In that case I can recommend something: an Australian film, *Debbie Down Under*. Believe me, it has some funny moments, and her timing is impeccable. Or there's always a classic, the adult version of *The Odd Couple*—that's very funny, trust me."

Diane just stared at him. Who was this intrusive man who appeared to have seen every pornographic film ever made? He moved closer to her.

Diane looked away. Now he was bothering her. He seemed to be assuming something about her. She hated that, hated when people thought that they knew her. It was intrusive. Like this guy. He started to hand her yet another video when she saw his wedding ring. That did it.

"Would you like to go to a movie?" she asked shyly.

He smiled, not at all surprised by the invitation. "Here's my card. I can't go now, but I'd like you to call me, and yes, let's go to a movie sometime." He went to the cashier, paid for his three rentals, and left.

Diane watched him walk out the door. She read the card she still held in her hand:

Joe Della Femina
Plumber
657-0944

"This could be my lucky number," she thought.

Later on in the week they had dinner at her place and sat in front of the fake fire. "Why are all the decent men always married?" Diane asked herself as he unhooked her bra.

They worked out a code so Diane could phone Joe at any time, day or night, even at home. When Diane called, if a woman answered, she was to hang up immediately, and if a man answered, it was probably Joe.

"I've never been made love to by a plumber before," said Diane, gently stroking his forehead.

"I've never been made love to by a—I don't even know what you do for a living."

"I'm a therapist. I also run a group called Brave Women and—oh, I don't want to talk about this."

"Okay, sorry, I just wanted to know all about you," he said. "It seems like you know everything about me and I don't know anything about you."

"Yes," she answered. "That's exactly right."

three

The following Sunday night, Diane hurried into her office at five after seven. "Sorry I'm late, everybody. Let's start the meeting right away please." Suddenly, as she was apologizing, it seemed to Diane that there was an extra source of light in the room tonight. She turned toward it, and her eyes were suddenly assailed by the brightest shocking-pink polyester pantsuit Diane had ever seen. Squinting, she ventured, "You must be Estelle."

"Yes, thank you," Estelle gushed. "May I smoke?"

Diane froze. "Well," she fumbled, looking around, "since our numbers are small tonight I think that would be all right."

It was true. Tonight there was only Carla, Judy, Kyle, Missy, Estelle, and Diane—hardly enough to form half of the W.

"Well, Judy and Kyle, we missed you last week. What kind of sofa did you pick out?" asked Diane, finally taking her seat.

Kyle and Judy searched each other as if to ask who should answer. Finally, Judy spoke. "The truth is, we couldn't decide. I wanted a nice floral print and Kyle preferred a black leather couch. So we compromised and got a futon, which neither of us wanted."

There was applause by everyone but Estelle. "What the hell is a futon?" she demanded.

The group turned to Estelle and stared at her cigarette. Carla coughed and tried to wave away the smoke. They turned their irritated gaze to Diane, who, she realized, was expected to say something.

"I think I made a mistake, Estelle, when I said you could

light up," said Diane. "And I think that the group would prefer if you didn't."

Estelle promptly stomped out her cigarette and took a
nicotine patch out of her purse and applied it to her forearm
as the others watched in horror.

Estelle spoke. "Does anyone care for gum? It's
Nicorette."

Missy shrank in her seat. Her mind raced with ugly
thoughts concerning Estelle. "I hate her with all my heart,"
she thought. "I've never been so clear on anything in my
life, except that I'd love to kill this shimmering woman."

"Missy? What do you think?" asked someone.

Missy was nonplused. "I'm sorry, I wasn't paying attention. I was just remembering some things I had to get done.
Sorry, would you mind repeating the question if it's not too
much trouble?"

The group stared at Missy, uniform in their sudden
shock at the visual travesty before them. They were so busy
absorbing Estelle no one had noticed: Missy had a new haircut since last week, the worst any of them had ever seen. It
was a cruel dose of reality, completely sobering to the half
W. No one wanted to say what they were thinking: that
Missy looked like she was sitting underneath a Polynesian
thatched-hut roof.

Estelle stopped chewing for a second (she had already
coped with Missy's haircut) and said, "Maybe if you
stopped daydreaming and started living in the real world you
wouldn't be such a burden to this delicious group of young
women!" Estelle looked at these ladies. They were so young
it took her already limited breathing capacity away. She felt
immediately isolated from them because of their youth.
They were all in their prime, and she was not. These women
assumed that she was less significant than they were because

of her advanced age, she was sure. "What I wouldn't give to be twenty years younger," Estelle thought, peering at Diane's unlined face. "If anyone ever deserved another crack at youth, it's me."

Diane stepped in. "I think, Missy and Estelle, that both of you have some issues, issues concerning yourselves as women," she said, "but this is neither the time nor the place for—"

Kyle let go of Judy's hand and said, "This exactly the time and the place!"

The others agreed vehemently. Estelle was just relieved that the two women had stopped holding hands.

Diane became very flustered. "I...you're right! I don't know what I was thinking. The truth is...well, never mind...it's not important. I guess I just felt like having—I apologize to the group!"

Judy spoke up, nodding eagerly. "Thank you, Diane. It takes a lot of courage to own up to feelings like that."

Kyle took Judy's hand and gave it a supportive squeeze. Estelle winced.

Carla raised her hand.

"Yes, Carla?" said Diane, still shaky.

"Let me get this straight: if something about another group member bothers us, we're allowed to tell them?"

"Well, yes," said Diane.

Carla looked slowly around the room at each member, took a deep breath, closed her eyes, and said, "Okay, I just wanted to know. Thanks."

Diane exhaled, disappointed. Like the other women, she was hoping to find out more about Carla. "Not tonight, I suppose." She turned back to the issue at hand. Diane looked at Missy, stripped of her dignity by a thoughtless hairdresser, and gently said, "I'm sure that you must have a few unsettling feelings after what Estelle said to you. Why don't you get them off your chest?"

The group turned to Missy.

"This is impossible," she thought. "How did I get into this situation? If I say what I really think to Estelle, there would be too many complications. Todd might get mad, Estelle might get even meaner, if that's possible, which, knowing her, I'm sure it is." Missy remained wordless as the rest of the women waited. For her, honesty came at too high a price, always had. She had never learned to deal with the inevitable consequences that followed standing up for herself. It was more than she could shoulder. She knew that because she had blindly tried it once, without thinking about it. Missy was still in high school and lived alone with her mother. Her father was no longer with them, having "died a saint", according to her mother, some years earlier. On the day in question her mother expressed an opposing opinion as to which dress Missy should wear to the prom. It was followed by the words, "Your dead father would have liked that one...I know."

"Yeah," Missy answered, swept away by the beauty of the dress she preferred. "But this one's so pretty!" She turned from the frilly prom dress back to her mother, who's face had now become a masterpiece of martyrdom.

"No, Missy," said her mother quietly, "wear the other."

"I thought you always told me it was unfeminine to say no," said Missy, still looking adoringly at the dress.

"I'm not the one saying 'no'," explained Missy's mother, shaking her head, "It's your father. He's the one. I'm simply speaking on his behalf. But if you think you know his taste in prom dresses better..." Then she began to cry. Soft, small sobs, so that Missy had to strain to hear, which she found herself doing, even after her mother had left the room.

Missy wore the plain dress that her mother—no, her father, had chosen.

To this day, Missy could still feel the relief she encountered when her mother finally stopped crying. To go from fearing that the one parent you had left had withdrawn her love, to having it back again, all within the space of an hour, was quite an emotional trek. Missy realized she was responsible for her mother's happiness. She knew because her mother whispered it in Missy's ear the night of her prom, right after she told the teenagers, "Have a good time." Missy accepted the responsibility. It seemed harmless. And it made her mother so happy. For Missy, it just always seemed easier to disappoint herself than to disappoint others.

"Missy," said Diane, "Are you okay?"

Suddenly Missy was back with them, and was expected, at this moment, to speak. She saw Estelle and felt the fear well up. The other women were smiling kindly at her, sympathy and support oozing from them. "Maybe I could say something," she thought, "I'd hate to disappoint these ladies." Finally, she spoke, "Well," she admitted slowly, painfully, "it's not the easiest thing in the world to confront your own mother-in-law, especially in front of people. But...I guess..." Just then Missy got a much needed nod from Diane, enough approval to continue. "I would sort of kind of maybe like it if you would stop being so...why don't you just...live and let live?"

The group immediately turned back to Estelle. Every shimmering thread on her suit was still. Finally, she returned fire with a single sentence: "My husband left me!"

Diane stepped in, eager to shield Missy from as much pain as she could. "Estelle, why don't you share your feelings with the group? We're cur...I mean, we care," said Diane. "Go on."

"Well, if I could get a word in edgewise" she announced, and promptly removed the Nicorette gum from her mouth in an effort to gear up for her lengthy tale. She shifted in her seat, rearranging her vividly-wrapped legs, making the others wait as she paused a full sixty seconds with hand on chest to let a small belch pass, which she then blamed on Missy's cooking. Finally it was all systems go. "My husband left me two months ago. Needless to say I got the shock of my life. I was raw emotionally, and I admit I became addicted to NyQuil."

"I didn't know that," said Missy.

"That's because you're always wrapped up in your own little dramas!" snapped Estelle. "You've seen my recycling, you didn't notice a whole bag full of empty NyQuil bottles?"

"It must have been before you moved in with me and Todd," said Missy.

"Well, as a matter of fact it was, but thank God I learned that I was a finalist in the Publishers Clearinghouse Sweepstakes and that gave me the strength to pour my NyQuil down the drain. You take courage wherever you can get it."

Group sentiment was now inching toward Estelle.

Missy sighed. Somehow Estelle always managed to talk about Estelle.

"Our problems started when Todd Senior—that's my husband, wanted to retire and move to Texas. I told him no! I won't go, I don't have the hair to live in Texas. Plus, I don't want to be away from Todd Junior—that's my son. I know he'd miss me too much and I couldn't do that to him. So my husband left me and moved."

The ladies waited for more but Estelle's body language (she quickly put the Nicorette gum back in her mouth) told them that this was the end. The group was disappointed, not in the story itself (although most had to admit it was not nearly as meaty as they had hoped), but because Estelle refused to delve beyond any surface feelings she might have had about her husband leaving.

"She'll learn to open up," thought Diane, who sensed that they should just move on to another problem for now.

They spent the rest of the meeting listening to Judy and Kyle talk about being in a brand new relationship. The ups, the downs, knowing when to compromise, learning not to drag their own baggage into a relationship (Judy's ex-husband, whom she left for Kyle).

"This could kill me," thought Estelle, who had never in her wildest dreams ever believed that homosexuality really existed. "I always thought it was something made up by Hollywood."

"Judy, I'd like to bring something up but I don't want you to get mad," said Kyle.

"Oh God," thought Estelle, "if it could upset her, think of what it could do to me."

Judy nodded and seemed to brace herself, as if she already knew what Kyle was going to say.

"When we were in the grocery store-"

Judy cut her off. "I'm sorry, I shouldn't have done that. I just got scared, I panicked, I didn't know what to do."

"That wasn't so bad," thought Estelle, quietly priding herself on her new-found liberal attitude.

"I understand," said Kyle, "but I can't tell you how hurt I was."

"I know," said Judy quickly. Too quickly, Kyle thought. It was two weeks ago that they were doing their grocery shopping and Kyle noticed that Judy seemed to be hurrying for no reason. Then, when Kyle took Judy's hand Judy took it back. It was then that Kyle noticed that there was a man looking at Judy.

"Judy chose not to introduce me to her sophomore biology teacher," Kyle announced to the rest of the group, aware that they had been waiting patiently in the dark.

"Oh my God," thought Estelle, "I'm smack in the middle of Peyton Place!"

Judy turned to Kyle. "He wasn't my high school teacher. He was my ex-husband's brother. I lied."

A hush fell on the room.

"I figured," said Kyle. She hugged Judy. "Believe it or not, I understand." She did, too. It had taken Kyle half of her life to accept her feelings for women. She had been where Judy was now, and she wouldn't wish that confused state of mind on anyone.

"I don't deserve you," said Judy, "I…I lied to you."

"You did the best you could. Trust me, I know."

Judy thought about that. She realized that Kyle was right: at the time, she did do the best she could. It was the first time that they had run into anyone that Judy knew from before, and she had panicked. Now it seemed that Kyle was telling her that it was understandable. She went on to forgive herself.

They both cried and acknowledged that things weren't going to be easy for them. They also decided to return the futon and get something they both wanted.

Missy was riveted. Though she hardly knew them, she liked Judy and Kyle and was impressed with their relationship, particularly with Kyle's empathy. Impressive, too, was the fact that Kyle wasn't threatened by the lie that Judy told. "That's a strong person. In fact, they're both strong," she thought, her own weaknesses swelling in her mind. "They have equal voices. I never thought that was possible in a relationship. I thought one had to be a leader and one a fol-lower."

"Does anyone else have anything she'd like to throw on the table before we call it a night?" asked Diane.

Judy and Kyle, still holding hands, raised them in the air.

"Yes?" asked Diane.

"We'd like to invite everyone to a ceremony," said Judy. "It's not a wedding per se, but it is a formal celebration of our newfound love. We are dedicating ourselves to each other." "It's also BYOB," added Kyle.

"Can I smoke or should I bring more skin patches?" asked Estelle, earnestly.

"You can smoke," said Kyle after a nod from Judy.

"Well, that's it, unless there's anything else?" asked Diane, looking around the room.

For a split second Estelle thought about raising her hand to throw something of her own on the table. Almost in the same instant that the desire presented itself, however, she squelched it completely, stomping it out like one of her lip-stick-stained cigarette butts. Estelle was already unnerved just by being here, in this room, with all these raw feelings, not to mention wood beams, exposed. Estelle decided that she would keep her real pain far away from these nosy women. For her restraint, she was proud. "It's enough com-fort for me to sit back and judge these whiny women. That's all the therapy I need."

"Okay," Diane continued, "See you all next week. Remember, stay centered, welcome your own inner child with open arms, and know that it's okay to admit you're frail as china, because," and everyone but Estelle (who didn't know the words) voiced in unison, "That's what Brave Women do!"

four

Every Mother's Day Todd Junior noticed a sick feeling in his gut accompanied by a slight death wish. "What is it about the first Sunday in May that bothers me so much?" he wondered, year after year. "Obviously something unspeakably horrible happened to me on that day and I've blocked it out."

Todd also noticed that same malaise creeping up on other specific days of the year: January second was hard for him, but there was nothing unusual about that day, maybe because it was deep into winter and winter was his least favorite season. "Thank God it's also Estelle's birthday," he thought, grateful for the built-in distraction. Whatever it was, he was sure that if he ignored the problem it would go away. It had to, because that feeling was becoming almost unbearable and he felt afraid that he would snap one day. "I can't afford to be distracted because I've got that big interview with the Post Office coming up," he thought. He closed his eyes and tried not to think about the beginning of May.

•

Joe Della Femina was in the middle of installing brand new pipe for Yelena Helgit, his oldest client. She was in her early eighties and she adored Joe. Every time he came to work she showered him with food. She cooked elegant, grand lunches, served on her best china, just like she used to prepare for her father in the old country. Mrs. Helgit was originally from a small principality within Slavonia, a tiny country in Eastern Europe. The land of her birth was called Kebashnik, and its main export was sausage.

The Kebashnik people, or Kebashniks, as they were

called, were on the short side. Yelena Helgit in her prime was only five feet, and currently, at age eighty-two, she stood four-eleven. Her red hair, the pride and joy of her youth, was now gone, shabbily replaced by matted white strands that seemed to barely cover her scalp. Her eyesight was bad, which was somewhat fortunate, because Yelena couldn't see the countless age spots that now cluttered her once clear complexion. Today, sitting across from her plumber, she flirted shamelessly with him, and hoped that he found her as attractive as she did him. Yelena talked endlessly about her homeland: all the colors of the native foods, the Paprika Festival in the summer, and the many suitors that fought over her when she was a young girl with "cheeks like apples."

Mrs. Helgit had many suitors indeed. She had outlived three husbands—two Kebashnik natives and one from Cleveland. But the one she spoke most about, the suitor that always brought tears to her eyes and even more of a tremor to her hands than there usually was, was named Slak Yorvik. He was one of the few men that she had never married, much to her lifelong regret.

Joe had heard the story of how they met about a billion times and was about to hear it again.

Mrs. Helgit was working in a fish factory. She was just twelve, but the laws and customs were different in Kebashnik. They placed a high value on child labor. Mrs. Helgit took a sip of pungent wine and began her story. "It was a bright, sunny winter day in Kebashnik..."

Joe reached for his unusual beer stein (it had a working clock on the side) and settled in for what he knew would be a long story. The up side was that he charged by the hour and felt no guilt whatsoever about billing Mrs. Helgit for her stories. "So go ahead old lady," he thought, "ramble on."

"I was walking to the factory. The winds carried with them the smell of fish and sausage. Traveling ahead of me on foot was a boy wearing the most beautiful hat. I knew he was royalty because in Kebashnik a hat was the sign of royal blood. Commoners were not allowed to wear any kind of a hat, no matter how cold the winters got. The more tassels on a hat, the more important the family. His had only a few tassels, but the colors were so brilliant in the morning sun. I was just looking at his bright headgear, counting the tassels, when suddenly, he turned around and smiled—at me! Oh, I smiled back, then I looked away, because that's all a young girl was permitted to do in Kebashnik before marriage."

"Later I found his name to be Slak Yorvik, and he too worked at the fish factory. Every night I prayed to God that I would be the one he would take as his bride. But I knew it could never be so, for a royal was forbidden by law to marry a 'Krukyuk' or commoner, and that's what I was."

Mrs. Helgit's eyes were starting to water now. Joe checked his beer stein for the correct time. He had to be careful, because he had a date. Then he had to get home to his wife.

●

Tonight Diane wanted to look especially alluring for her evening with Joe, though they were just going to do the same old thing: eat dinner at Diane's place and then make feverish, noisy love. They were literally two prisoners in a high rise. After a year of "staying in," Diane was desperate to see Joe's face against a different backdrop—something other than the off-white walls of her one-bedroom apartment.

She was going to be thirty-nine years old soon, and needless to say Joe was not interested in trying to "get pregnant."

Diane studied herself in her bedroom mirror and wondered, "How do I bring up marriage to a married man?"

five

The Brave Women meeting was just coming to order. Kyle and Judy were there, radiating a happiness few people could even fathom.

Missy and Estelle were there, radiating a hatred for each other that only a mother and daughter-in-law could share.

Carla was there, passing out pictures of her Shar-pei taken in a nondescript setting.

"Are you by any chance part of a witness protection program?" asked Kyle, searching the picture for any kind of clue.

"Yeah, that's right," said Carla. "I'm here every week at the exact same time spilling my guts to you people at the risk of being found out and killed." Carla rolled her eyes in disgust but the group never saw it because she was wearing dark glasses.

"Women comforting women is something I'd be willing to die for," said Judy, smiling at Kyle. The group was chipping in on a wedding present for the happy couple, who were registered at a local sporting goods store.

"Are we allowed to bring our husbands to your wedding?" asked Missy

"Of course, bring anyone you'd like. This is a day we'd like to share with everyone," said Judy, beaming.

"Good, then I'll bring Todd," said Missy and Estelle, at the exact same moment.

They glanced at each other.

"Look, it's getting late and we've got a lot of complaining to do, so who'd like to go first?" asked Diane.

"I've got something I'd like to talk about," said Judy, letting go of Kyle's hand. "I'm going to close my veterinary practice. It's time I made a change in my life."

"Leaving your husband for a woman wasn't enough of a change?" Diane wondered, privately.

Judy continued. "I've decided to go to medical school!"

Estelle's hand shot into the air. "Judy, sometimes, whenever I'm in a room with air-conditioning I develop an awful rash. What do you think it is?"

"I'm not a doctor yet," said Judy, slightly annoyed.

"Judy, I think I speak for the group when I say I think that's wonderful news," said Diane. Everyone nodded.

"Just remember," Diane continued, "when your life becomes a chaotic nightmare, and you begin to doubt the very essence of your being, you can always come here and lay your weary head on our collective bosom."

Kyle cleared her throat.

"I mean that figuratively of course," Diane added quickly.

"Look," said Judy, "I know that medical school is going to be the hardest thing I've ever done, but for the first time in my life I feel that I could actually get through it. And I think that most of it stems from the love I get from Kyle, but I also think that some of it comes from being a member of Brave Women."

Diane led them all in applause.

Estelle, miffed at the attention Judy was getting by simply rambling on and on about herself, addressed the group. "When I was younger I had goals similar to yours; I wanted to marry a doctor. I didn't though...I married a Protestant."

The group was confused. Kyle offered Estelle some mint snuff, which she declined by shaking her head and waving it away.

Diane stifled a yawn. "Feel free to flow, Estelle."

Estelle did so. "You see, I didn't love Todd Senior, but

my mother did. She demanded that I marry him. And, as you know, I did, although Todd Senior is nowhere near a doctor—he's a television repair man."

"*Was* a TV repair man. He retired," corrected Missy.

"Well, I think you've found a wonderful outlet for your anger: your mother," said Diane.

"It's been done before," said Missy, softly, almost to herself.

Estelle turned on her daughter-in-law, thinking that the reference was aimed at her.

"Let me ask you something: have you ever experienced a man placing his seed in your womb to carry and nurture, to ripen and mature so that it flows out of your body in a moment of miracle?"

"No," answered Missy.

"Then I suggest you refrain from commenting on anyone's relationship with their mother when you haven't the guts to become one yourself."

Silence. No one rushed to Missy's defense. Each woman seemed to be cowed by this statement in much the same way that Missy was.

At that moment Estelle realized something wonderful: she was currently the only one in the room that had given birth. None of the others had! My God, they must have realized it too. How they must admire her! And resent her. No, she wasn't a veterinarian like Miss Know-it-all, she had never had a career like women nowadays, but she had done the most important thing anyone could do: go forth and multiply. Why hadn't she thought of it before? Now she had something on them, now she could feel as important as they thought they were. Hell, she was much more of a woman than any of them. After all, that is what it means to be a real woman, Estelle knew. She was back on top, no longer threatened by the others. It was a marvelous, liberating feeling. In an instant Estelle went from skeptic to wholehearted supporter of group therapy.

"Tell me, Estelle," asked Diane, "you don't exactly strike me as the maternal type yourself. Do you think you became a mother in an effort to please your own mother?"

There was quiet. Finally, Estelle spoke. "No," she said, "if I had wanted to please my mother I would have had a girl."

When Estelle and Missy returned home, Todd was standing in front of a sink full of dishes wearing an apron that said BORN TO CLEAN on the front.

"Don't forget to wipe your feet—I just washed the floor," he called as they were coming in. "How was the meeting?"

Estelle took off her patch and lit a cigarette, eyeing the green and yellow kitchen with disgust. "It was, as they say, a meeting."

"Dad called," said Todd, rinsing a plate. "He wants you to call him. I said I didn't know if you would. Missy, could you hand me that glass please?"

"Did you have to say it out loud?" asked Estelle. "You couldn't have whispered it in my ear?"

●

Estelle Rogers almost came from money. Her parents lost their capital during the depression. Lyle Delrose, Estelle's father, was addicted to gambling and literally lost all of the family money in poker games. That was in 1928. Grace, Estelle's mother, was devastated. They had planned to move to a bigger apartment, maybe even a house. Now that was no longer possible. They were stuck in four cramped rooms with a baby on the way. It was the beginning of the end of their marriage. A few months later, when Grace's father had died unexpectedly at ninety-seven, she and Lyle inherited ten thousand dollars. Taking no chances, Grace immediately put the money where her lousy husband couldn't gamble it away—in the stock market. She felt at ease for approximately one month, and then the day before the crash hit, Lyle found out where the stock certificates were, forged her signature in order to sell the stock, and then bet it all on a horse named Lucky Grace. He lost.

Five months later Grace gave birth to a baby girl. The two most popular baby names in the country were Estelle and Alma. Grace named her child Estelle Alma Delrose.

Lyle and his wife never had another child because Lyle and his wife never had sex again. Grace hated the sight of her husband. She never got over not losing their money in the stock market like everybody else. Grace hated being different. That's why she gave her daughter names that were popular. She wanted her daughter, Estelle, to blend.

Life was bleak in the hot apartment above the Italian bakery. The kitchen faucet was rusty and there were worn, peeling linoleum floors everywhere, even in the bedrooms. Estelle's mother never paid much attention to her, too busy saying the rosary or spewing venomous declarations of hate at her husband. Once, Estelle did see her mother actually trying to strangle her father with her black beaded rosary.

They lived across the street from a funeral home, Mortimer's. It was where Estelle's father went to work when he lost his job after the crash. Business was booming and they needed the extra help. They were expanding, three waking parlors now. Somehow, to Estelle, her father's job seemed glamorous, like he was always hosting big parties for people who were all dressed up. From her bedroom she'd watch all the people go in and out of the funeral home, talking and laughing and crying. It all seemed so alive to her, compared to her own house where no one really spoke. It was definitely an out of the ordinary occupation, special, even, which gave Estelle something to hook on to. Something to deflect some of the dreariness of her life.

Later, as a teenager, Estelle resented her mother's disdain for her father. She rejected her mother's "neurotic need" to be average. So followed Estelle's lifelong passion for shiny clothes—anything that made her stand out in a dark room. Soon she went to work as a secretary for the phone company but was let go because her work clothes were deemed "inappropriate" for the everyday. As she was being handed her severance pay, Estelle once again asked why she was being let go when her work was impeccable.

Her supervisor responded, "The outfits. Gold lamé is hard on the eyes under incandescent lights. You stick out. This is the phone company, not a night club. Hey, there's an idea for you—why don't you go answer phones in a night club?"

That's just what Estelle did. She got a job at the Gaslight Club as a waitress. The uniforms were gorgeous—red beaded and strapless. Estelle eventually worked her way up to hostess, seating people. It was a job meant for her, the lights, the glamour, the abundance of second hand smoke. That's how Estelle got hooked—she got addicted to the smoke-filled air and that was it.

Estelle was hosting when Todd Rogers walked into The Gaslight Club. He had just moved from Texas and wanted to eat at the best place in town. He took one look at Estelle and asked her to marry him. She thought he was rich because he was from Texas, and Estelle took him home to meet her parents.

She had to introduce him twice due to the fact that her mother had vowed never to be in the same room as her father. Growing up, Estelle's mother warned her not to marry because, "all men are subconsciously trying to harm us." She changed her tune with Todd, though, when he brought her flowers. Soon, Estelle's mother told her to marry Todd Senior because, "if another depression comes you can always move to Texas."

They married and went to Texas on their honeymoon. Estelle hated it. It was big and green and bright. She was used to dark, smoky rooms and crowds. And oh, was it humid! Estelle hated what humidity did to her raven hair. She vowed never to go back, and they never did.

six

Pam Bender, a client of Diane's, but not a member of Brave Women, hurried into Diane's office. She plopped her tall frame down in the chair opposite Diane, and seethed. "I hate him! He's definitely cheating on me!"

"Wait a second, take a breath, release your anger, and calmly tell me what's happened," said Diane, putting away her *Bride's* magazine.

"He's not the man I married anymore." She shifted her body, and shook her head. Pam took that deep breath that Diane had prescribed. When she deemed herself able to carry on rationally, Pam continued, calmly, determined to make her point. "We used to 'do it', any time, any place, day or night, no questions asked."

"Why on earth would you ever need a therapist?" asked Diane.

"Because lately that's changed. He doesn't want 'it' like he used to," she sobbed.

Boy, have you got problems, Diane thought. "Listen, Pam, last time we spoke you mentioned these same issues and I urged you to confront your sexually gifted husband. Obviously, you didn't ask him straight out if he was cheating on you, like I told you to."

Pam stopped sobbing. "Yes I did! That's why he won't touch me. Now I made him angry because you told me to say something! It's all your fault. Before, at least we had incredible sex. Now I'm stuck with an Italian man who won't touch me!"

Diane leaned in, eager to comfort her now celibate client. "On the surface, this is bad, I'll admit. But don't you feel just a tiny bit better having confronted someone who is so obviously cheating on you? Is that what you, as a woman, are willing to settle for—a husband who lies and cheats?"

Pam inwardly weighed the pros and cons.

Diane grew visibly impatient.

"I guess you're right," Pam conceded.

"Why don't you tell me exactly what happened," said Diane.

Pam sat up straight. "Well, you know he's a plumber."

Diane felt a little warm.

"And he had just come home from an all night job fixing sewer pipes reeking of Chanel Number Five. So I said to him 'Honey, you didn't spend the night in a sewer, did you? You were with some cheap, bottled blonde!'"

"Easy. His mistress might be a very attractive, together woman," Diane offered.

Pam stared at her. "You're my therapist. Don't defend the slut that he's using for sex."

"How do you know he's using her?" Diane asked.

"What?"

Diane defended her statement. "I'm just suggesting that we women should stick together and you should remember that your husband is the one who's cheating. He's the one who promised to be faithful to you in what was probably a big, lavish church wedding. Try not to lash out at just anyone because she's an easy target."

"What do you think I should do?" asked Pam.

"I think you should consider leaving him," said Diane.

Pam was quiet for a long time. "I can't leave him. I'll never leave him because I adore him more and more with every breath I take."

"That's not much of a reason to stay with someone," said Diane.

"Oh," said Pam. "How 'bout this: I'm pregnant again."

"Better."

Diane raced home after work and studied the picture of Joe and his wife and kids on her dresser. Because they were wearing Old West costumes, Joe's wife had a hat on with a black netted veil over her face. Frankly, it was hard to tell what his wife looked like. Diane examined the photo until her eyes hurt. She determined that the woman in the black and white photo was not her client. Diane poured herself a glass of low-calorie white wine and had a seat at her kitchen table, still holding the picture. Deep down, Diane knew there was no way that Joe was this woman's husband. She blamed her paranoia on the fact that she was currently menstruating (happy to have a concrete medical explanation), and to the fact that she was having an affair with an Italian plumber. Maybe it was the wine, but right then Diane decided she would take her own advice: confront Joe and demand that he leave his wife, whoever she was.

seven

Todd Junior's interview with the Post Office was a snap, he decided. The lie detector test was a breeze. Mostly they just asked him routine questions: had he ever used drugs, or pulled out an Uzi in a shopping mall. "No," answered Todd politely, somewhat bored. "I'm a people person," he offered brightly, waving to the gentlemen behind the two-way mirror. Todd knew it was a two-way mirror because he had been arrested once.

The questions continued. "Have you ever watched Court TV and fixated on any man wearing a bow tie?" asked the man administering the test.

Todd thought for a moment. "No."

"If you were to 'end it all' one day, would you be content to go it alone?" the man asked, taking a bite of his lunch.

"Yes," answered Todd, smelling the man's juicy roast beef sandwich.

"Do pretzels taste salty to you?" asked the interviewer, slowly moving his sandwich from Todd's covetous gaze.

"Yes," Todd said.

"Were you ever aware of deriving an abnormal amount of pleasure when you watched the television show called *Bewitched*?" he asked.

"No," answered Todd, choosing not to reveal that he had built a shrine to Marlo Thomas during her *That Girl* years.

"Do you think Theodore Kaczynski got a raw deal?" the man inquired, wiping beef juice from his chin.

"Nn...no," Todd replied.

"Do you like baseball?"

"No."

The interviewer stopped eating and looked into the two-way mirror, then continued, a little more cautious. "Have you ever had a perm?"

Todd stopped a moment and ran a sweaty palm through his dark, curly hair.

"Ummmm...no."

The machine made a noise.

"Yes!" he said quickly.

"We're almost through. Would it bother you to be brow-beaten and brainwashed by a superior for the sole purpose of getting one more letter there on time?" asked the interviewer, looking at his watch.

Todd sensed that this answer was important. While he was thinking pictures were flashing in his mind, vivid momentary images of his glittering mother whispering in his ear and then laughing, wildly. Then a memory of the third grade spelling bee he lost, remembering how he told his mother what a raw deal he got from the judges.

The interviewer cleared his throat.

Todd hurried back from his trip down memory lane. He assembled a big, eager smile on his face, and answered the question to the best of his knowledge: "No."

"Welcome to the Post Office," said the interviewer, offering Todd what was left of his sandwich.

eight

At the end of the Brave Women meeting, Carla asked if she could have a word with Missy.

"Is she mad at me?" Missy wondered. She quickly got angry at herself for entertaining such a paranoid thought. Missy looked around the loft and found it empty except for Carla. And herself, of course. Missy forgot she was there too. It was a habit she had, forgetting that she, too, was in the room.

"I've written down the name and number of a woman I know who cuts hair," said Carla, tactfully. "She really knows what she's doing." Carla knew she was making Missy nervous, putting her on the spot, but she couldn't help it, this was something that had to be done.

Missy looked at the piece of paper Carla had just placed in her hand. "But...I don't think...it's just..." Missy stammered.

Carla waited patiently for Missy to finish, whenever that might be. One thing that she was learning at Brave Women was how to be a good listener. She also found that she liked Missy and wanted to help her. Someone had to.

Missy eventually gathered her thoughts and her nerve. "I-I don't know if I can let someone cut my hair besides my regular hairdresser, Marie. I-I'm afraid."

Carla smiled. "I thought you might say that. This is my reply." She simply held up a small mirror in front of Missy and watched her face fall. "I'm sorry," said Carla, "but I had to do it. It's called tough love. It was either this or a complete hair intervention by the group at next week's meeting."

Missy looked down at the phone number in her sweaty palm, then back at Carla. "I'm sorry. I just...I'm afraid she'll get mad at me."

"But Missy, what can she do to you that she hasn't already done to your hair?"

"Missy," said Carla, gently lowering her already low voice, "please trust me. I've known Carol since high school. She cuts all my wigs—she's very good!"

Missy promised Carla she'd think about it and the two said good-bye. In the following days Missy kept her promise to consider her hair options. In fact, to her dismay, she could think of little else. "I know I have the right to choose any hairdresser I want, I just don't have the right guts. I don't have any guts. Hairdressers are mean. What if she hears through the grapevine that I've gone to someone else? She'll start badmouthing me to everyone. And they'll have to listen! They'll be stuck in the chair while she goes on and on about me." She felt weak—sick, in fact. Although she had to admit to having a new feeling: she was touched that Carla and the rest of the group cared about her that much. She was flattered by their attention. It both moved her and unnerved her. A few days later, Missy decided to risk Marie's wrath and get herself a new hairdresser.

Carol took clients in her home. Missy drove slowly down the street looking patiently for an address, finally locating the house. She parked the car and cautiously walked up to the blue frame dwelling, which was curiously covered in cobwebs. The bushes appeared white under the sheath of cottony dew. Missy was taken aback. She parted some of the web around the doorbell and rang it. Moments later a sunny, cheerful woman answered the door and welcomed Missy. "Hi. I'm Carol. And you are?"

Missy answered quickly. "I'm Carla's friend Missy? Are you the Carol that does hair?"

"Yes, I am. I've been expecting you. Would you like to come in?" she asked airily.

Missy was hesitant but entered the home. She looked around and was impressed. The inside of the house was amazingly clean, and Carol's own hair was beautiful. It was cut short, wispy brown bangs framing an attractive face. She had a crisp, sporty appearance, of the type which Missy had always admired from a distance, never daring to dream that she herself was capable of pulling off such a look. Missy followed Carol into the basement where she had her hair salon.

Carol washed her client's hair and started to cut. Missy's eyes were closed and she was beginning to relax when the whispering from the other room started. Missy opened her eyes quickly.

"What's that?"

Carol smiled sweetly and said, "I have twin teenage daughters. I'm sorry, let me go ask them not to bother us. Excuse me."

Missy relaxed again. Carol was so nice. Just as she picked up a hair magazine to distract herself, she heard three whispers. She leaned in the direction of the voices. They were right behind the door that must have led to the family room, because Missy could hear muffled television noises. Above them she heard Carol whispering, "Don't be silly, I'm just giving her a trim. All right, now stop this, you're embarrassing me."

Carol came back and apologized. "I'm sorry."

"Is everything all right?" asked Missy.

"Oh, it's nothing. They just wanted some of your hair but I told them no. Oh good, you found that magazine," said Carol.

"Why on earth would they want some of my hair?"

Missy asked.

Carol giggled. "They're interested in witchcraft and Satanism. You know teenagers—it's always something," she said, shrugging her shoulders.

Missy stared at Carol snipping away at her hair and noticed the door. It was cracked just a little, and she saw four heavily made-up eyes peering at her.

"I…" Missy started to speak but couldn't. She wanted to say in no uncertain terms that they were not to get any of her hair. The thought of those kids using her own hair for Satanic rituals was frightening. Suddenly she wished she was back with Marie, her old hairdresser. At least with Marie Missy knew what to expect, even if it was bad. This was so different! This was the road less traveled, and it was scary. No wonder women kept going back to their abusive hairdressers, again and again. It was the fear of the unknown. "God only knows what she'll do to my hair!" thought Missy. She realized that now, however, there was no escaping saying the word no. Now she was forced to speak up for herself, something Missy would rather go to Hell and back to avoid. She silently confirmed what she already knew she had to do. "Now I have to make it clear that I don't want my hair used in any kind of Satanic ritual because some of my split ends are already on her floor. If I don't say anything she'll just give my hair to her kids after I leave." She looked directly into the face of the model on the cover of the magazine in her lap and confronted Carol. "I don't…"

"You don't want them to have your hair?" asked Carol, just as sweet as could be.

"Yes!" uttered a relieved Missy, proud of herself for taking the bull by the horns.

"Relax, I'm not taking enough hair to fill a witch's pouch. That's all they want it for," smiled Carol.

Missy relaxed. She even felt a little foolish for getting upset.

"Would it bother you if they used a little for their altar?" Carol asked earnestly.

"Y-yes, I'm afraid it would. Sorry." Missy wondered why she was apologizing. "Carol?"

"Yes?"

"I don't want my hair to leave this room. In fact, when I leave, I want to take it with me, if that's okay."

"Oh sure," said Carol. "Listen, I understand. I'll tell you, between their witchcraft and driving them to The Gap I don't have a moment to myself! You'll see when you have your own teenagers."

Missy stared at this nice woman chatting airily in front of her, going on about her daughters' interest in witchcraft and Satanism as if they had just joined the high school glee club. "Talk about denial. This is how I'll end up if I don't learn to say what I'm feeling, if I'm always afraid to say no. Especially if I'm afraid to say it to my children," she quietly considered.

When Missy fought her way back out of the cobwebs she had a new haircut, a new attitude, and a jar full of hair. Well, it was the *beginning* of a new attitude, actually.

nine

Yelena Helgit was canning sausage for her plumber, Joe Della Femina. She was worried about him. She noticed that lately he seemed restless when she talked about Kebashnik. Often during their lunches Yelena caught Joe checking the glassware for the time. "He must be worried about getting back to my leaky pipes," she thought as she pressed the meat into the tin can. "After all," she considered smugly, "I'm quite a storyteller!"

Yelena might have included the words "long-winded" in her heady self-assessment. Often, she had thought of writing her tales down so "the whole world can share in the glory of Kebashnik!" As she finished up her canning, she noted bitterly a book on the kitchen shelf. It was by Isak Dinesen. Yelena had an ongoing love/hate relationship with the Danish author. She could not help but admire her literary gifts, but Yelena maintained that Isak had really been born in Kebashnik, and emigrated to Denmark later on. And, because she was ashamed of Kebashnik, pretended that she had been born a Dane. "She's ashamed of her own homeland!" For years she wrote to Isak, begging her to use her notoriety to bring tourism to Kebashnik. The letters all came back, unopened. But Yelena knew. She knew it was just a woman turning her back on her people. Yelena now cast her thoughts to her immediate concern: how to get Joe to stay for lunch after he had worked on her pipes.

Yelena often spoke to Joe about her first love, Slak Yorvik, but she didn't tell him the whole truth: that Joe looked so much like Slak that they could have been brothers. To her he was the spitting image of her many-tasseled suitor. Ever since the first day that she had met Joe. She still couldn't get over it.

Actually, the real truth was that Joe Della Femina looked nothing like Slak Yorvik. Joe's caveman-like body, hairy and muscular, blue eyes, set off by a constant tan, was more opposite Yelena's love than similar. As a young man, Slak Yorvik was five feet four inches tall, with small bones and the narrowest of hips. His skin was fair, so light in fact that it appeared translucent in spots. Slak's head was large, and where there should have been hair, there were veins. Still, when Yelena looked at Joe, it was Slak she saw.

Yelena felt twelve all over again. She could smell the fish factory, especially when she was very close to Joe. She remembered Slak's gentleness, and how different he was from other Kebashnik men. In her country, the males were not raised to be kind to women, it just wasn't part of their culture. Somehow, Slak was different; why, she didn't know. He had always been sweet, and yet when he wanted to marry her she had answered no. Now he had come back to her. There was no letting go of this plumber, she would see to it. His bills were enormous, but Yelena paid no mind; for she had found her precious Slak once more, and she would not make the same mistake this time. This time they would marry.

ten

Estelle was beginning to miss her husband, but told no one. Who would she tell? Todd Junior? No. That wasn't what only sons were for. He was her immortality. Todd would be here long after she had met her maker. She couldn't risk him remembering her as weak or weepy. That would be, as they say, unacceptable. Estelle knew for a fact that Todd thought of her as strong and dynamic. He must have—she had gone to great lengths, made great sacrifices, all his life, to see to that. At school plays, she was always the best-dressed mother in the audience, the one the other parents constantly turned their heads to look at as she took her seat, sometimes even long after the play had begun, their faces registering looks of obvious envy, masked, Estelle knew, behind their snide, sophomoric snickers. Children needed an exceptional role model, Estelle knew that. She personally had given her only son…well, herself, really.

When Estelle was expecting Todd, she was struck by the theories of a certain child psychologist who recommended that parents allow their children to worship one or both parents. That desire to idolize was a "natural, primal instinct" in children, he claimed. "Don't discourage it. It's good for them. It will make them feel safe." This made sense to Estelle. She herself was the daughter of a somewhat cowardly father, who gambled as a way of relieving stress. He was weak. Even as a child Estelle could sense it. It left her with an empty, isolating sense of despair inside. His constant fear, Estelle would always remember, had a ripple effect, often spilling over onto her and spoiling what should have been a carefree, depression-era childhood, causing Estelle to take a vow of controversy later on in life. She would never be afraid to speak her mind, she swore it. She would not, under any circumstances, become like her father, who always ran from confrontation, refusing to yell even at the ice man when he left blocks of half-melted ice for their chest. And Estelle would not be like her mother, who embraced the ordinary, so as not to be noticed. No, Estelle decided that she would always be a dynamic force in her child's life, allowing herself to be viewed as a maternal icon, even, if that's what it took to ensure a normal, well-adjusted son. It seemed reasonable to her, it made sense. How else did children learn but by example? Estelle had always been a glittering, shining example for her male offspring. She was tough and she knew it. Hers was always the most feared voice at PTA meetings. But she was also a giver. Estelle perpetually spouted the most demanding, insistent cheers at Todd's fifth grade basketball games. She tirelessly screamed out the most demeaning, humiliating rhymes when the opposing team of ten-year-olds made a mistake, rubbing their runny little noses in their own misfortunes from her perch high in the bleachers. In fact, the year that Todd was on the team they won all their games, most players having admitted privately to their mothers that they were afraid to lose in front of Estelle.

Yes, she decided, she had done a marvelous job raising her son. That's probably why he had married such a mousy excuse for a wife. Why on Earth would Todd need a strong wife when he had his mother?

Estelle had never been a victim of feelings the way Missy was. Estelle had no use for them. Their purpose was never obvious to her. Certainly, people had them, but why let them affect you? Even at Brave Women, she was proud of the way she kept her feelings, at least the ones that counted, bottled up inside, giving her the right to inwardly claim confidence over those social snivelers. Estelle swore to herself that she only went to those meetings so she could keep an eye on Missy, for Todd's sake.

"I don't want her saying anything that could embarrass him. Oh God, that daughter-in-law of mine," she mused as she browsed through Neiman-Marcus one afternoon. Literally surrounded by endless racks of evening gowns, Estelle was visually reminded of Missy's outstanding lack of style.

It was true. Missy's fashion sense was neither here nor there. Often, she would wear the same clothes two days in a row without realizing it. Estelle considered this a personal affront to her.

In fact, Estelle regarded Missy as the current source of all her troubles. Missy's mere presence, in a way, caused Estelle to privately question herself. Ever since Todd had married her Estelle had begun to feel self-conscious. Even though she never said a word, Missy made her feel silly about her taste in clothes, for example. And, though there was no question that Estelle's taste was, and always would be, impeccable, it bothered her that Missy dressed so plainly. It was as if, simply by breathing, Missy caused Estelle to ponder her overall sense of identity. This was something that Estelle had thought that she was through with: any form of self-doubt. But now, even the volume at which Estelle spoke (loud and booming) made her feel out of place, somewhat, because Missy always spoke in such a quiet monotone.

"I hate quiet people," she thought, making some sort of stab at an explanation as to why Missy consistently rubbed her the wrong way. "I don't trust her, the Irish one. She's always so suspicious of people. She won't let anyone help her. When will she realize that Neiman's is on her side? Saks is not the enemy—they only want to guide her! She always fights the wonderful saleswomen who only want to make her look as delicious as she can!" Exasperated, Estelle threw her hands in the air, causing an obsequious salesgirl to come racing over.

"May I help you?" she asked excitedly. Estelle looked at the eager-to-please face in front of her and thought, "I'm home."

•

"Guess what!" shouted Pam Bender, waltzing triumphantly into Diane's office. "I was wrong! He wasn't cheating on me after all. He told me that when certain chemicals mix together, like the chemicals they use in the sewer mixed with certain aftershaves, they can resemble familiar smells, like Chanel Number Five, White Shoulders, even alcoholic drinks. I feel so much better."

Diane stared at her. "And you believe this?"

"Yes!" said Pam quickly, as if anticipating her skepticism.

The two women were silent. Finally, Diane could wait no longer. She proceeded cautiously, trying to soften the harsh sting of the truth. "Gullible Gussy!" she said, and made a face.

Pam's eyes narrowed. "How dare you judge me, you who are without husband. At least I've got a man of my own! I don't have to take someone else's."

Diane wasn't sure what she meant.

"I know about your affair. You think plumbers don't talk?"

Diane now knew what she meant. Quickly she tried to envision her client in an Old West costume, wearing a hat with a netted veil. "This is ridiculous!" thought Diane. "I'm getting paranoid again!"

Pam continued. "There's talk all over the sewers about you and some plumber!"

"First of all," said Diane, "if you must know, yes, I'm seeing someone who happens to be married AT THE MOMENT! In the second place, you bringing up my life just lets you avoid your own problems, and believe me, *you've got problems!* And thirdly, we have to decide together if your husband's lame excuse is the truth. I think you should stop burying your head in the sand and take a good, hard look at your life."

The two women sat looking at each other, each sensing that this was good advice for both of them.

●

Estelle and Missy sat waiting for Todd to come home with his news, wondering what it could be.

"How do you like my new outfit? Isn't it just delicious?" asked Estelle, standing and turning, ever so slowly, to allow her daughter-in-law to drink in her brand new gold lamé stretch pants and matching poncho.

"Oh, it's nice," Missy forced herself to say.

"I got it today at Neiman's. They asked about you." Estelle smiled as she puffed away.

Missy's insides turned. Every time Estelle came home from a shopping trip to Saks or Neiman's, she always said, "They asked about you." It was Estelle's way of trying to get Missy to buy the kinds of clothes that Estelle wanted her to buy. Thank God Todd forbade her to let Estelle force feed gold-plated clothes to her.

"I didn't have time to get my hair done—do you think Todd Junior will notice?" asked Estelle.

"It looks fine, but I know someone that could take you on short notice if you want to go now," she offered, picturing Estelle's hair being offered to, but ultimately refused by, Satan.

"Oh, God no. Todd will be here any second—I can't wait to hear what this big surprise is!"

Missy was feeling the same as Estelle, which in itself was quite frightening.

Estelle studied Missy. There was something different about her, but she could not put her finger on it. It was driving her crazy. "Missy?" asked Estelle, "Have you started smoking?"

"No," Missy answered, startled. "Oh, I think you're just noticing my new haircut. Do you like it?"

Just then, they both heard the key in the deadbolt.

"He's home!" said Estelle frantically stomping out her cigarette and running toward the door.

Missy stood to greet her husband. She was used to always being the second woman Todd kissed when he got home.

"Well, what's all this about wonderful news?" asked Estelle.

"I got a job at the Post Office!" said Todd, removing his clip-on tie.

"What about the airline?" asked Missy.

"He was probably tired of it!" answered Estelle.

Missy and Todd looked at Estelle.

Estelle misinterpreted their annoyance for interest in her opinion.

"I think a new career is a delicious idea! In fact, anything Todd wants to do is all right with Mama."

Todd noticed that same feeling welling up in him. That inexplicable malaise that he couldn't pinpoint the cause of. Pictures started to flash quickly in his mind again. Pictures of Mother's Day cards and guns. "I understand the gun part, that's probably very common," he thought to himself. "But why greeting cards?"

Todd stopped suddenly in the middle of his self-examination, unable to take his eyes off Missy. She noticed him looking at her new hairdo, and blushed.

He didn't say a word. He simply took Missy's hand in his own and led her up the stairs to their bedroom.

"Todd, how do you like my outfit?" Estelle asked. "Todd? Todd?"

Estelle continued to demand their immediate return. They didn't hear her. Or didn't seem to. Missy searched Todd's face for any sign that he was going to respond to his mother. There was nothing, and she realized that he wasn't going to. She couldn't believe it, he was putting her first in his life, for the first time. He was carrying her farther and farther away from Estelle's screams. To Missy, suddenly Estelle's distant, unanswered shouts had become a powerful aphrodisiac. She saw her husband in a new way. She looked into his eyes and melted.

Immediately, they embraced. Todd was all over Missy like one of Estelle's cheap suits.

"I better get my diaphragm in," whispered Missy. But Todd would not let her go. "Please," she insisted, "I'll just be a second."

Todd only kissed her harder, and finally, she gave in, forgetting about the diaphragm altogether. They abandoned themselves to the moment. "Just like on the soap operas," Missy thought.

eleven

The Brave Women all took their seats and looked for Diane's sympathetic smile, but there was none. She wasn't in the room. Estelle, Missy, Carla, Kyle and Judy were present, but no Diane. This was definitely a first. Suddenly, a voice began.

"Why don't we get started?"

Every head turned toward the voice except for Missy; mostly because it was Missy's own voice. "Did I say that?" she thought to herself, looking at everyone looking at her.

She spoke aloud again. "I'm sure Diane will be here in a minute. In the meantime, does anyone have anything intimate she'd like to expose to the group?"

The whole half-W stared at Missy. This was a side of her they hadn't seen, not to mention the flattering new haircut. Carla privately beamed. Judy and Kyle nodded to each other.

"Who died and left you boss?" demanded Estelle.

"Honestly, I don't know. I...I'm kind of surprised myself," she discovered.

Estelle eyed Missy cynically. The others had startled smiles on their faces. They were happy to see this new side of her. Each deliberated privately as to why Missy looked different. It wasn't just her hair. Something about Missy seemed so...fulfilled.

Just then an uncharacteristically haggard Diane came walking into the meeting, shaking her head, cursing the on-going road construction.

"Boy do you look awful!" said Estelle. The others, alarmed by Diane's suddenly poor posture, agreed.

"I'm sorry I'm late. Fortunately, I haven't been sleeping

at night so…"

"Fortunately?" asked Carla.

"Did I say fortunately? I meant unfortunately." Diane looked around distractedly. "So, um, what's going on?"

"Oh, you missed it," said Estelle. "Missy thinks she's Hillary Clinton." Estelle expected everyone to laugh with her and no one did.

Kyle announced excitedly, "Missy took over for you, Diane! She led the meeting."

The rest of the group gladly nodded their heads, except for Estelle, who yawned openly.

"Thanks, Missy, I appreciate it," offered a scattered Diane, who didn't seem capable of taking in the obvious enormity of the situation in her current, deteriorated state. "We're here to reinforce and to help each other because…that's what BRAVE WOMEN DO!" said a haggard-looking Diane, collapsing wearily in her chair.

Judy raised her hand and indicated that she'd like the floor. Missy nudged Diane, who quickly opened her tired eyes. "Yes? Who'd like to…"

"I would, please," said Judy, talking only with one hand because Kyle held the other. "Well, remember when I told you all that I was thinking of going to medical school?"

Estelle started to ask for free medical advice again. Judy noticed and spoke quickly. "Well, I won't be going to medical school after all," she said directly to Estelle. Then, turning her head to the rest of the women she announced, "Kyle and I are going to have a baby!"

The group was stunned. Estelle took out a nicotine patch and applied it directly over another patch on her forearm.

Missy thought for a brief second. "That means, if your baby is a boy, when he grows up and gets married his wife will have *two* mothers-in-law."

Kyle and Judy nodded.

"What if I had a catered baby shower? As soon as I find out who's pregnant," said Estelle, "I'll order a cake with the mother's name on it."

"We're both going to be mothers," said Judy. "But physically, I'm the one we both chose to carry the baby."

Despite their joyous revelation, Diane's mind was wandering toward her own life, her own problems. She was scared to bring up marriage again to Joe. She was frightened that he would leave her and find someone else to cheat on his wife with. She loved him. For the most part she believed that, believed that she loved him, at certain times more than others—when she watched a romantic movie on television, when she saw a child playing on the sidewalk, but mostly during the quiet emptiness of a Sunday night after the meetings. Every once in a while, however, something tugged at Diane, a feeling that she was not able to put into words. A notion that she was forgetting something whenever she was with Joe. What was it?

"Well, congratulations!" said Diane, rejoining the conversation at hand. "I can't tell you how happy I am for both of you!"

"Listen, Judy, I've got the most delicious silver rhinestone maternity dress, and I'd love to see you in it. In fact, I've got about forty maternity outfits from when I carried my Todd."

"I'd love that, Estelle," lied Judy. "Thank you."

Carla, silent this whole time, was somehow invigorated by the news. In a split second, Carla stood up and said, "Here's to life outside the womb!" and immediately tore off her large dark glasses.

The ladies were shocked. They had never seen Carla

without sunglasses. The group scrambled to finally see something of Carla's face before she covered it up again.

"I've got some eye makeup in my purse if you're interested," offered Estelle.

"She doesn't need it, she's got beautiful eyes," said Kyle. Judy quickly turned her head. "I-I just mean, why do you hide them behind glasses?" Kyle asked quickly, noting Judy's glare.

"Well," said Carla, "I'm not comfortable revealing who I am just yet. I'm not sure why, I think I don't want anyone to know I belong to a women's group."

"Why?" asked Missy.

"That's a very good question."

"Thank you," said Missy.

"And I'd like to answer but I don't know if even I know the answer," said Carla.

"Just tell us this much," asked Diane, "Is Carla your real name and are you running from the law?"

"Oh my God!" said Estelle.

Missy, patting her new haircut asked, "Are you hiding from a Satanic cult?"

"No," laughed Carla. "Look, I'm not a fugitive, I've never even had a traffic ticket, I swear."

"Then why all the mystery? Why do you let us bare our souls and you bare nothing?" asked Diane, herself a little miffed.

"Are you now or have you ever been a member of the communist party?" asked Estelle.

"No. And my name is not Carla. Look, I've revealed as much as I'm comfortable with tonight. Let's just say I came to this group to learn how to be more open. I'm going at my own speed. I…I don't seem to have the confidence that you all seem to."

Each woman privately savored those last few words.

"Well," smiled Diane. "The important thing is that you are here, and you are loved and accepted for who you really are, whoever that may be."

Carla held up her dark glasses to the group and broke them in two.

Swept away in the passion of the moment, Estelle rolled up her sleeve and tore off the double layer of nicotine patch. "I've come a long way baby!" she yelled, tossing the drained patches in the air.

In the chair across from Estelle sat Missy, on whom, unfortunately, the patches landed. She didn't notice, however, because she was engrossed in her thoughts. She was pleasantly re-living the beginning of tonight's meeting, and how good it felt to be a leader for once, and not just a follower.

twelve

"Have you been phoning my wife?" asked Joe, walking into Diane's bedroom.

"Of course not!" she said, putting the lid back on her new Nature's Way Honey 'n' Plenty o' Placenta Rejuvenating Cream.

"Well, someone has," he continued, dismissing her denial. "My wife said some woman called and said that I was in love with her."

"Well, I didn't do it."

Joe started toward her. "I gotta tell ya Diane, I'm not sure I believe you."

"I swear to God I did not call your wife."

"Come on, Diane."

Diane turned away, and began to rearrange the different moisturizers on her dresser. "Look, if I wanted to tell your wife about us I certainly wouldn't call. I hate talking on the phone."

Joe reached out and pulled Diane's left arm, knocking her most expensive night cream out of her hands. It fell on the glass nightstand next to the bed, its greasy contents spilling all over page seventy-six of her *Bride's* magazine.

"Well that's a hundred and twenty-five dollars down the drain. Thanks." Diane stopped for a moment as she allowed a thought to register in her mind. She turned and expressed it to Joe. "I just realized something: I don't care if someone called your wife, in fact, I'm glad someone finally brought it up. And as long as we're on the subject, I'd like to know what her response was. Is she going to give you a divorce?" She held her breath.

"I can't afford a divorce. She's threatening to take me to the cleaner's if I leave her."

"Talk about a sore loser!" Diane said. It started to feel like Sunday night to her—that emptiness in the pit of her stomach. Diane was ashamed that he didn't want her, but more ashamed of the way she felt inside. "Unattractive, unlovable, the usual clichés," Diane thought wearily, tired of the same old issues. She turned her head so he couldn't look at her. Her eyes focused on the picture of the smiling bride in the magazine, the one with the moisturizer spilled on it. Everything in the photograph was covered except for the bridal veil and the smile. "Life is so easy for some women..." Diane had to stop, because this line of thinking was making her out of control, which she certainly didn't need right now. "Honey, I don't care if we don't have any money. I just want to be married."

"And I just want things to stay the way they are," replied Joe.

Diane looked down. "Will we ever get married?"

"Don't I always come through for you? Don't I?" he asked, coming close. Too close. The ceiling fan blew his aftershave in all directions, making it impossible for her to think clearly. And his hand on her breast didn't help. She fought hard to remain conscious.

"I'm going to break up with you," she uttered breathlessly. "You'd better find a way to make some extra money so you can marry me. I want more than anything to become a repressed housewife."

"All right, when I get some extra dough, we'll get married," he promised. "Just don't call my wife anymore."

thirteen

Missy and Todd were just saying good-bye. It was Todd's first day of work at the Post Office, and he didn't want to be late because of the severe penalties involved. Todd didn't mention them to Missy because "methods of punishment are not to be talked about among civilians" was how his superior put it.

Missy admired her husband in his uniform. She noticed Todd had had most of his perm cut off recently and was now beginning to show some gray. "It's very becoming," she thought as he put on his coat.

She was starting to fall in love with her own husband. Ever since the night that they ignored Estelle in favor of making love. Right after that he started asking her opinion on things—he never really had done that before. It was usually Estelle he turned to. Just a few days ago he even said the words, "I'm sure whatever you decide will be fine with me."

Missy went up to Todd and gave him a kiss good-bye, in the middle of which a flash bulb went off right in their faces.

"Surprise!"

They both turned to see Estelle with a big blue dot covering her face, a pleasant side effect from the flash.

"Mom! We didn't want to wake you," said Todd, squinting.

"Truer words were never spoken," thought Missy.

"I wouldn't miss your first day of work! Honey, I hope it's just delicious!" said Estelle, beaming in a rhinestone shower cap and bathrobe. She reached in her pocket and took out a very long cigarette and lit it quickly. Estelle took her first puff as if it were a life-saving asthma inhaler.

"Well!" she said, not at all recognizing the irritation written all over the faces in front of her. "Tell me all about it!"

"I have to go," said Todd. He turned to walk out the door, but stopped, and turned back to Missy, pulled her close to him, and whispered in her ear, "Are you going to do what we talked about?"

Missy, stunned because this was the first time anyone in this house had ever whispered in her ear, simply nodded, too shocked to speak. Estelle watched in horror as her son whispered in another woman's ear. She started to choke on her cigarette. Missy and Todd immediately rushed to her.

"Are you all right, Mother?" asked Todd.

"What do you care, you're all wrapped up in your career anyway!" shouted Estelle as she went back upstairs, coughing all the way. "You go to your Post Office! Don't mind me, I only gave you life! You drained my body of calcium, and now you think of me only when a doctor asks about your immediate medical history!"

"Good-bye Missy," said Todd, surprising her again by not giving in to Estelle's tantrum. "I just CAN'T be late!"

And he was gone. And now Missy was stuck with an overdressed smokestack. Missy thought about what Todd had just whispered. The thought of it sickened her more than Estelle's cigarette smoke. She hesitated at the stairs, guessed at how Estelle would react to what she was about to say to her, and started up.

She quickly retreated to the kitchen. Missy needed more time to prepare her nervous system for what was about to take place.

She considered what Todd had asked her to do. It made sense—she just wasn't sure she could go through with it.

"If you don't do it, I will," a new and improved Todd had told her before he left for work. "I just think it would be better coming from you. It'll be good for you."

Missy didn't understand what was happening with him. Technically, this wasn't his first day of work at the Post Office—he had completed two weeks of training. And since then he was different. She noticed he had less tolerance for Estelle now, and whenever he had worries he didn't shut Missy out. The best thing about the new Todd, Missy noticed, was how irritating it was to Estelle. Missy secretly reveled in all of it—Estelle's shock at Todd's newly-found independence; his new maturity; his whispering in Missy's ear now instead of his mother's. The bad part was that Estelle smoked twice as much now—patch or no patch. Which brought Missy back to Todd's request: that she ask Estelle not to smoke in the house.

"How am I ever going to say that to Estelle?" she asked herself, trembling, yet thrilled at the same time. Somehow, the fact that Todd told her to do it made it easier. Also, Missy wasn't quite sure yet, but there might be another reason to put an end to Estelle's second-hand smoke.

She pondered as to the best way to go about this, the way that would make it easiest for Estelle. Suddenly it hit her: Missy would announce it first thing, right as Estelle was lighting up a cigarette with a cup of coffee because that was the one she enjoyed the most. "I'll tell her while she's in a good mood," she decided. Missy sat down at the kitchen table, relieved at having come up with a workable plan. Missy didn't have long to wait. Five minutes later her mother-in-law charged into the kitchen and fished through a drawer for a pack of matches.

Missy closed her eyes.

"Estelle?"

"What?"

Eyes still shut, nervous system alerted, she dove head

first into the cold, harsh, unforgiving waters. "Todd and I have sort of decided that we would prefer it if you didn't smoke in our house. It was Todd's idea."

Estelle looked at her Plain Jane daughter-in-law, and realized that life, as she had known it, was no longer. It may have been a small thing, what they were asking, but it really meant that they didn't respect her anymore, no longer feared her (the two had always gone hand-in-hand in her mind). It meant change, something that had always unraveled Estelle. "Change is sneaky," she maintained, her coping skills being somewhat arthritic and dusty at this point. "Adapt" had forever been a four-letter word in her consciousness. Estelle had always dismissed anything new because it meant letting go of something else. Change meant that the past was past, over, dead and gone. "How in God's name could the death of something be good?" she always had wondered. "I'll bet this *was* Todd's idea," Estelle decided. "Of course it doesn't matter. It's done and that's that." She'd be damned if she was going to let them see it affect her. At least she had that option, which seemed to be the only one open to her at this point. And now, looking at Missy slouching nervously in front of her, she realized the awful truth: Missy and Todd were on their side of the fence, together. She was on hers, alone.

The two women stared at each other. The bright, sunny kitchen became dark with hate. Estelle moved slowly, contemplating her options. Obviously, the Democrats had taken over the White House. The power had shifted for some unknown reason and Estelle silently went over strategies in her mind.

Missy looked at the beaded turban on her mother-in-law's head and knew that beneath the jeweled cotton wrap wheels were turning. Old, rusty wheels. Her stomach clenched in anticipation. She was ready for any and all abuse that Estelle would surely heap on her, for she was sure now that Todd would protect her. "Let me have it," thought a brave Missy.

"You know something," said Estelle, "that's a good idea!"

And with that she took her long cigarettes and promptly threw them away. She then turned and walked up to her bedroom, leaving a shell-shocked Missy all alone in the kitchen. Missy turned and went to get the bread for toast and realized that her hands weren't shaking as much as she had anticipated. She had been fantasizing about this exchange for days and days, coming up with scenarios that played out very differently than the one she had just lived through. The ones in her head frightened her and they always ended the same way: with Estelle undercutting her statement and then laughing at her. But that didn't happen. Instead, amazingly, Missy was aware that she felt just the tiniest, smallest bit…sorry for Estelle.

Upstairs, Estelle quickly threw on a pair of metallic slacks and a matching blouse. She pounced down the back steps, walked silently past Missy, out the back door and into her Mazda. Estelle pulled out of the driveway with no particular destination in mind. As she sped away, she reached desperately for a cigarette and finally lit up. Estelle slowly, deliberately sucked in the smoke, and silently thanked God she was alive.

She turned on the car radio and searched for some music. Her hand stopped for some reason at one of those Chatty Cathy stations, as Estelle called them. She heard a talk show host giving advice to a first-time caller—a sympathetic young male nurse. Estelle listened intently while puffing away.

"It's the hospital's word against mine," said the nurse.

"Uh-ha," was all the radio host would say.

"I didn't forget to turn on the oxygen tent! Obviously somebody else came and turned it off," insisted the man. "It's ridiculous," he continued. "I became a male nurse to help people, not to kill them. Look, even though the hospital has assured me that they supposedly won't jump to any conclusions and not to worry, just between you and me, I feel like I'm being persecuted. Do you know what I mean?"

"Do I ever," thought Estelle.

The radio host was clearly out of his league and had no idea how to respond. The caller took that as a sign to keep talking.

"See, we've had a rash of deaths at the hospital where I work..."

"DON'T say the na..." screamed the host.

"St. Mar-BEEP-nas," he said, not having heard the radio host. The engineer was sure he had bleeped it out in time. People at home were desperately trying to figure out which hospital it was, which wasn't all that difficult, seeing as how St. Martina's was the only one in town.

"And I can tell you right now they are all errors on the side of the hospital, things like giving the wrong patient a mercy killing. One patient died because there was ground glass in his oatmeal, and it was too bad, too, because he had just come out of a ten year coma and was just starting on solid foods—which is part of the reason he didn't notice the glass. I just can't hold any of this in any more—I feel like I'm ready to burst and I don't know where to turn. I feel like no one will believe me."

The radio host had been given three warnings to get this guy off the air but their switchboard was lighting up like never before—mostly it was people from St. Martina's legal department. "Well," he fumbled, "I guess we'll call you the White Knight. And I thank you for calling. I wish you the best of luck and I pray I don't need to go into the hospital!"

"Look, I'm sorry, I know that I probably sound like a real oddball, but I'm not."

He stopped for a moment.

Estelle reached for the knob and turned the radio up.

"Did you ever feel completely and totally alone?" asked the caller.

"YES, I have," remembered Estelle. "Once. A long, long time ago."

"See, my whole life, I've seen things one way, through the eyes of a nurse's uniform. That's all I've ever wanted to be. That's the only way I've ever seen myself. Now, if they take away my license to be a nurse…it's a cliché, but it's true: I won't know who I am anymore. How am I supposed to change now? I'm thirty-five. How am I supposed to redefine myself at this age?"

"Looks like we're out of time," announced the relieved host.

"Thank you for listening," said the White Knight. "I'm sorry if I took up a lot of time. I want you to know how much I appreciate it. I don't have any family."

"Me neither!" screamed Estelle. She turned the radio down, the voice of the White Knight still dancing in her consciousness. As she drove, she replayed his hospital stories over and over in her mind, not really sure why, but aware that the sound of his voice gave her pleasure. Was it his voice? His stories? Was it the fact that when he spoke there was just a hint of isolation, of loneliness that came through over the airwaves? Everything in Estelle wanted to hold the body that was attached to that voice, to mother him. She wanted to put her arms around him and tell him that it was all right, even, some would say, fashionable, to cry.

Estelle had never felt so intimate with someone before. Suddenly she felt close to a person who was physically miles away. Luckily for her she did not see the irony— Estelle hated irony, felt tricked by it, and would roll her eyes in disgust whenever it was pointed out to her. For right now, Estelle sat alone in her car, haunted by a voice that seemed to need her.

fourteen

It was late in the evening. Yelena Helgit was sitting by the phone in her boudoir, having a glass of Yanyavik, the native drink of Kebashnik, made from one part prune juice, three parts vodka, and a splash of sour cream. Yelena loved them late at night, although sometimes she even treated herself to one in the morning, after the mail had come.

Midway through the third Yanyavik, Yelena made the call to Joe's wife. Had she waited until the fourth Yanyavik, she would not have been able to dial the phone, and Joe's wife would never have suspected a thing. And because Yelena was delightfully crocked, her normally thick European accent was distorted and slowed down, in the end sounding very much like a sexy older woman from Atlanta.

It was Yelena's drunken intention to get Slak to marry her. They both knew that he wasn't coming over to fix her pipes.

Remembering back to his last visit she noticed that he didn't have his many-tasseled hat anymore. "Maybe he threw it away in protest," she thought. "Or maybe he forgot it somewhere. I'm not the only one who's getting old."

Taking another sip of Yanyavik, she had forgotten making the call already. She picked up her dusty book of photographs and began looking at the old pictures. Most were taken in Kebashnik when she was still a young girl. Yelena let out a big squeal as she saw the picture of the day she skinned the most pigs at the annual Paprika Festival. She was standing in front of a brightly painted barn holding up a sack full of skins. She thought back to that day, and because she was remembering it through a happy haze of alcohol, she grew nostalgic for her youth. There were other pictures to look at. The day she played the accordion at her uncle's funeral—that was a day she remembered with great pride, for she had only had four lessons before that, but was assured that she played beautifully. Oh, how Yelena longed for her youth, to relive her childhood in the fish factory. The fun they had changing shifts! The tricks they played on the guards, stuffing fish heads into the barrels of their guns! Teasing the killer dogs at lunch time. And oh, seeing who could climb the barbed-wire fence the highest! Yelena grew sad as she remembered, not for the obvious reasons, but because she was old now, and the only things that made her feel young anymore were Yanyavik and Joe, the plumber.

●

Pam Bender was talking to her therapist but Diane wasn't listening. She was looking at Pam's skin, wondering what kind of moisturizer she used. Diane knew she couldn't interrupt Pam's sobbing to inquire, but she made a note on her pad to ask at the end of the session.

"Blah, blah, blah," Diane thought as she watched her client go on for the billionth time about her husband. It was always the same thing: one week Pam was sure he was cheating on her. The next week she came in telling Diane that everything was fine, he wasn't cheating, and then she would repeat that week's ludicrous excuse handed to her by her husband. This week was the affair week. So Diane figured she didn't need to listen, she had heard it all before. She began planning an exotic meal for Joe to enjoy, trying now to remember if he said he liked anchovies.

"Are you listening to me?" asked Pam, blowing her nose.

"You were saying that the panties you found in the back seat of your car weren't yours."

"That's right. Sorry. I guess I'm getting suspicious of everyone. I shouldn't get mad at you. You're not cheating on me!" she sobbed. "I'm just paranoid ever since I was wrong about being pregnant. Now I think I'm imagining everything. Do you think I'm imagining that he's cheating on me?" Diane's mind started to wander again

●

In a dark room filled with elaborate, overly-ornate bedroom furniture, an old woman was dialing the same phone number for the fourth night in a row.

It was pure luck that Yelena managed to dial correctly, because her hands shook incessantly, which is one reason she had started drinking a Yanyavik every now and again. After two sips her hands no longer quaked, although somehow tonight they were trembling anyway, even after consuming an entire pitcher of Yanyaviks. She finally finished dialing and heard it ring. Yelena gazed at the ornate old telephone and was delighted to see two of it. Just as she was remembering that it was against the law for a commoner to own two telephones in Kebashnik, a woman answered.

"Hello?" she said.

"Youra husband..." Yelena started to doze, but was awakened by the woman on the other end.

"Is this you again?" said Joe's wife impatiently, "If you don't stop calling I'm going to report..."

"Youra husband and I will know the many flavors of Kebashnik," she said, and then promptly fell asleep.

The woman on the other end listened to the heavy, thick breathing and something dawned on her: "That's the labored snoring of a sausage lover."

fifteen

Pam Bender was upset when she walked into Diane's office.

"Good," thought Diane, "she's ready to work."

"I need to say something to you, Diane, something that I haven't had the guts to say before."

Diane got up and closed the door, never taking her eyes off her crying client.

Pam groped for the right words. "I can't kid myself any more—I know my husband cheats on me." She stopped, letting the words repeat themselves in her own mind, to be sure of what she had just said. "I-I'm divorcing him."

"Good for you!" Diane jumped right in.

"And I'm leaving you."

Diane looked up. "I've always hated those words," she realized privately. Yet on a certain level, whenever she heard them, they seemed to make sense, like they belonged in her life, and always would. "Of course, you're leaving me," she thought, "I'm not good enough, am I?" Diane couldn't squelch the bitterness in time, couldn't stop herself from saying out loud, "Why are you leaving me, Pam? I didn't cheat on you. Why are you punishing me?"

Diane quickly got a hold of herself. "I'm sorry, that was a really unprofessional thing to say...what I meant was, I know you're not trying to punish me, you're trying to punish your unfaithful husband, and I respect you for it. I'm just not sure that ending therapy is going to help. You might just end up punishing yourself."

Pam shook her head and paced. Diane didn't seem to be understanding this as readily as she had hoped.

"All I do here is talk."

"But that's how you do therapy," said Diane. "Isn't it nice to know that you do it well?"

Pam persisted. "I want to be on my own. I want to stop saving things up all week to ask your advice about. I want to start asking myself for advice. I want to start learning how to think for myself."

"I thought that's what you were learning here," said Diane, hoping the hurt didn't show in her complexion. "I also don't think you know what it means to be on your own."

Pam stopped. "That's the point, Diane—I don't. But I'm going to find out." Pam gazed at her attractive therapist, suddenly so sad, and said, "Look, don't think that this is easy for me. In fact I almost think it's harder to leave you than to leave my husband…it seemed like we had a better relationship."

Those words were like a cool washcloth on a sunburned face to Diane. She paused a moment to let them soothe her, grateful to Pam for saying them.

"Pam, anything you want to do, I'll support you in. Just as long as you're sure," Diane said.

"About the surest I've ever been in my life," she replied. "I don't know, maybe I just had some kind of moment of enlightenment or something corny like that, who knows?" Pam continued, " I just want this part of my life to be over. I want something better for myself. Do you know what I mean?"

Diane knew exactly what she meant. She stood up and held her arms out to her now ex-client. The two neurotic women hugged for a long time, each wishing the best for the other.

Diane was moody and quiet for the next few weeks. She wasn't sure why. Nothing could bring her out of it—not Joe, not a new antifungal moisturizer filled with promises—nothing. Her days seemed to stretch out endlessly in front of her, and the thought of filling them made her tired. There was something in the back of her mind that was bothering her.

Diane knew that she had been stuck at the same point in her head for years, but still, she couldn't find a way to give up the little bit of comfort she got from dating married men. She just couldn't make that leap. And now, even her own client was willing to take a tremendous leap of faith into the unknown, with two kids yet. Diane hadn't been aware of it before, but Pam's constant wavering was a big comfort to her. She subconsciously used it to help herself feel better about not doing anything about her own life. Now things were different. "But why?" she wondered. "Why now? I've been telling her to leave him for so long...I never thought she'd do it," Diane realized. "What happened to make her actually go through with it?" For a moment, Diane hoped that it wasn't because of anything that she had said, but quickly realized how silly that notion was. Actually, thinking that made it occur to Diane that perhaps she was Pam's catalyst, on a certain level. Maybe she was a good therapist, perhaps better than she gave herself credit for. But still, there had to have been something else to make Pam cross that line. What was it? She thought over and over about what Pam had said, about how maybe she had had a moment of enlightenment...

Diane decided that she would create a fake moment of enlightenment for herself. It was an honest attempt to bring herself out of her current state of sadness. Diane was aware that she was just pretending, that she didn't have the luxury of knowing that what she was about to say to Joe was absolutely right on the money, of knowing for certain that she wasn't making a mistake, but what the hell, if Pam Bender could make a change…

She gave Joe an ultimatum—marry me or lose me.

"I can't afford a divorce," he said.

"This isn't about money—either you think enough of me to marry me or you don't," continued Diane, feeling her way blindly, hoping that Joe would think she had suddenly seen the light in terms of her own self-worth. "And frankly, if you don't want to marry me, I'd rather face it now, not ten years and a dozen wrinkles from now." That last sentence, Diane was suddenly delighted to realize, she was sure about.

"I told you, when I get some money stashed I'll marry you, okay?" he said.

"Okay."

sixteen

A neighbor found Yelena's body slumped over a pitcher of Yanyaviks. Unfortunately, her hand would not let go of the handle because *rigor mortis* had already set in, so the ambulance drivers had to break the elaborate pitcher before they put her on the gurney. The coroner determined that this was not the first cocktail that she had mixed for herself. He concluded this not by fancy forensic methods, but simply by the smile on her face that was frozen there forever. She had no relatives to phone, she was just an old woman who lived alone, canning sausage that no one would eat.

•

Estelle bought a portable radio for her room. The White Knight was calling that radio station quite a bit and she was definitely hooked. It also took her mind off the fact that Todd Junior had become a stranger to his own mother. Estelle was still absorbing the fact that Missy and Todd had asked her not to smoke in the house. And that wasn't all: no more whispering in Todd's ear—that was a <u>direct</u> <u>quote</u> from Missy, via Todd, Estelle remembered bitterly.

It hurt to think about her decaying relationship with her only son, and so she turned all of her energy to the radio. She took off her beaded bathrobe and got into bed and tuned in the call-in show. Estelle closed her eyes for just a moment. Forty-five minutes later her sleep was interrupted by a familiar voice coming over the airwaves.

"I am planning on writing a tell-all book," said the voice. *"Confessions of a Male Nurse."*

Absorbing his voice, Estelle was energized. Every part of her was now awake and aware of a longing. She wanted so much to reach out and hold the White Knight. It seemed to her that this young man was just a pawn in a cynical bureaucracy and needed understanding and a hot meal. He was more sensitive than most people, which was probably why he became a nurse, thought Estelle, dying for a cigarette—patch or no patch.

The White Knight spoke again. "I know I'm probably going to lose my job at St. Mar-BEEP-na's, but this is important. I won't lie to you. I'm scared to think that I might lose my job, but you would do the same thing if you knew what was going on here."

The host of the show said quickly, "Please remember not to say the name of the particular hospital."

"I'll try to remember. I'm sorry—I don't want to get you in trouble—I'm just blinded by my own indignation and also a certain no-calorie sugar substitute. I have severe…"

"DON'T say the NAME!"

"…allergies to Equal…"

BEEP.

"And I'm better off if I personally don't have it, but I know a lot of people like it."

The host was starting to sweat again. "Look, White Knight, I gotta tell you, since you've been calling our ratings have gone through the roof, so on the one hand I'm really grateful, but please understand that one of our advertisers is the maker of NutraSweet, so if you don't mind, keep your opinions and your allergies to yourself."

There was silence. Estelle sat up, eager for someone to say something. Finally, the host spoke.

"Are you there, caller?"

"I suppose," the White Knight uttered slowly. "Sorry, I guess I thought that this was America—you know, freedom of speech?"

"What have you found out lately?" asked the host.

"Lately I've been looking at doctored x-rays." The White Knight waited for those words to sink in.

"What do you mean?" asked the host. "Like if I had an x-ray the hospital would make it seem like I needed an operation when I didn't?"

"Well...if it walks like a duck and talks like a duck..." he answered. "Let me just say this, you know how they can air brush things out of pictures, like wrinkles, moles, et cetera? Well, they can also put things in."

"Like?"

"Oh, things like they have an artist come into the lab and draw in fibroid tumors on the x-ray, badly, I might add. One artist even drew in the likeness of a dime in the intestinal cavity. The doctor told the patient that he must have swallowed a dime when he was little and it had to come out."

"And of course, the surgeon just pulled a dime out of his pocket and put it in a hospital jar after the operation, right? How would the patient ever know? Well, I guess he'd know if someone wrote a book and spilled the beans," said the host.

"Exactly."

"If I were you I would be very careful. Your life might be in danger. I wouldn't be surprised if there were people looking for you right now," said the host.

Estelle smiled, an idea having just occurred to her.

The next morning, when Estelle went down for breakfast, she noticed something different about her daughter-in-law. She didn't seem as...hollow, unsure, somehow. Estelle had no time for further contemplation, however. She was on her way out to the garage to smoke a cigarette.

"How are you, Estelle?" asked Missy, stopping her with her question.

Estelle was suspicious. She could smell a trap. "How am I? Well right now I'm having nicotine withdrawal symptoms. How are you?"

"I'm...having a baby."

"Oh my God in Heaven Hallowed Be Thy Name," replied Estelle.

"I can't tell—are you happy, granny?"

Estelle felt that word enter her body unannounced. It started in her brain and traveled quickly through her synapses before crash-landing in her flabby gut.

"Aren't you going to say anything?" asked Missy.

"Tobacco," was all Estelle could manage as she stumbled out the back door.

seventeen

It was the beginning of Autumn. As the members of Brave Women were making their way to the meeting from the parking lot, each could smell the scent of fires burning in fireplaces wafting through the crisp night air.

Diane welcomed everyone and suggested that they all get started as soon as possible. "Who'd like to begin?"

Estelle cringed as Missy raised her hand. "I have an announcement."

"Oh really?" said Diane.

"Yes, I'm going to..."

Estelle jumped in and said the words with Missy.

"...have a baby."

Missy glared at Estelle, who in turn just fiddled innocently with the nicotine patch on her arm.

There were cheers from the group, and a slight look of envy from Judy and Kyle, who were currently waiting to see if their attempt at artificial insemination had worked. They were, however, still happy for Missy and Estelle.

"That's wonderful," said Diane, who was also a little jealous because her biological clock was ticking fast.

"Estelle, you're going to be a grandma! Congratulations!" said Kyle.

Estelle could barely disguise her desire to trade places with Missy—so that she would be the one harboring and nurturing a new life and receiving envious looks.

The group was unusually quiet.

"Well," said Diane, "How do you really feel about being a mother? And I mean *really*."

"Well, of course, I'm ecstatic," sang Missy.

Diane knew there was more. "And..."

"And, well there's the obvious concern: will I be a failure as a mother?" she said, peering at Estelle.

Everyone nodded.

"I mean, I hope I can set a good example for my child." Missy sighed and looked down at the floor. She wasn't sure how revealing she could be in front of her mother-in-law. She didn't like to give her any ammunition. "Oh, what the hell," she thought. "I'm sick of censoring my responses because of Estelle." She looked back up to the group. "I just know from my husband's personal experience the severe damage that being a bad mother can do."

The others looked immediately to Estelle, who merely sat in her chair, pulling lint off her silver cape.

Missy, lost in her own painfully forthright admissions, didn't notice the group staring at her mother-in-law, and continued. "It's so important to be a good role model and...I know I'm not that strong a person. Sometimes I wonder if I'm anyone worth emulating, if I'm strong enough to be a good parent."

"Cry me a river," said Estelle, pulling the final piece of lint off her cape, never even looking up.

Diane addressed Missy. "I think sometimes, when we ask questions, the universe gives us answers. Sometimes they come in strange ways."

"You're saying that I'll get an answer to my question?" asked Missy.

"Probably," said Diane.

"Oh."

Missy sat, thinking, wondering how the answer would come. The rest of the group was quiet, each woman peering covetously at the expectant mother's stomach, every one of them willing to give her right ovary to be in Missy's shoes.

●

Kyle and Judy were in the living room sitting on the new couch that they had finally agreed on. It had taken months of looking, but they eventually spotted one. It was an overstuffed gray-and-beige-striped sofa, and both ladies thought it much better than the futon they had returned.

The television was on. They were enjoying a medical drama. Sprawled across both their laps was a work in progress: an enormous pink and blue baby quilt that Kyle had designed herself. She was an accomplished quilter and was currently teaching Judy the fine art. Now that the nights were getting chilly, it was particularly pleasing to both be huddled underneath the warm quilt, contentedly sewing away.

They had settled into a surprisingly comfortable routine since Judy had moved into Kyle's condo. Both had jobs that paid well, Kyle especially. She designed packages for generic products, but was currently interviewing at Quaker Oats, in the children's cereal division, for something that demanded a little more of her abilities.

The two were in love and content. Kyle had lived with women previously, but she noticed that the relationships had never taken on this effortless quality before.

Judy felt the same. She wasn't sure why, exactly. It was not as if she and her husband had had a bad relationship. Actually, life with her husband had been quite affable in a lot of ways...and sometimes, though she would never tell Kyle, she even missed him. He was funny, and had a way of making her feel...protected... that Judy was surprised to find that she missed. "Maybe that wasn't even it," she pondered. "Maybe I just feel so...exposed in my new lifestyle." It definitely made her nervous at times, and she tended to avoid certain acquaintances for fear they'd ask, "What's new?" But her unsettling feelings were few and far between compared to how she felt about Kyle. Judy knew that she had never been this way with anyone, male or female. In fact, that's what Judy found most strange. Their relationship didn't seem weighed down by gender, it seemed so beyond that, or above it. Whatever it was, Judy felt a closeness and a love for Kyle that she had never experienced before. This feeling in her life definitely compensated for any awkwardness a thousand times over. And it all happened so easily, that was the oddest part. When Kyle told her she had never been so relaxed in a relationship before, Judy understood. That was exactly how she felt. There was a simplicity to their love that made them both feel so carefree. "I just love the ordinariness of our life," she told Kyle one Sunday morning, as they were sealing the grout around the bathroom sink. "It's so…predictable, and I love it. Chinese and a movie Saturday night, Wednesday night Yoga lessons together, our health club..."

Kyle knew what she meant. It's not that they didn't have things to work on in the relationship (Kyle's impatience with Judy's guilt about leaving her husband, for example), but their life together, in the main, contained a good deal of serenity, certainly more than either one had known before. They enjoyed going to movies, taking walks, browsing in bookstores, applying each other's makeup…

Kyle looked up from her quilt block and noticed Judy's pained face. "What's wrong? Did you stab your finger again?" Kyle quickly handed her a Kleenex, so she wouldn't get blood on the quilt. Judy took the Kleenex, but she didn't apply it to her finger. She dabbed the corner of her left eye with it.

Kyle stopped quilting and secured her needle into the

fabric. Judy just sat there, staring down at the baby quilt that they had been working on. She started to cry. Suddenly Kyle knew. "You just got your period. We're not pregnant." Judy nodded. Kyle fumbled for the remote control and finally muted the television. The minutes passed in silence.

They both felt afraid, as if this failure was proof that they would never be able to have a child. Kyle had a friend who had tried artificial insemination twenty-eight times and it had never worked. This possibility was starting to loom over their relationship. They never talked about it, but it was there.

Kyle put her arms around Judy and they comforted each other, the way they one day hoped to comfort a child of their own.

"Well, now we don't have to worry about finishing the quilt in time," Kyle joked. Judy didn't laugh.

"Come on, let's go to bed," said Kyle.

Judy pressed the OFF button on the remote just as a young intern was finishing up an emergency Cesarean on a nineteen-year-old girl.

eighteen

Services for Yelena Helgit were brief. In Kebashnik, it was customary to wake the body a full two weeks in the nearest relative's home, each day draping the casket with a different flag of Kebashnik. There were exactly fourteen different national flags, each a brighter color than the last. On the final day of the wake, relatives always gathered in a circle around the body and together chanted the Prayer for the Dead in their native language. Translated, the prayer said the English equivalent of "It's been nice knowing you." There was more, of course, the overall gist of what was said being, "Your body is now dead and that's too bad for you." (The Kebashnik people don't believe in an afterlife—their basic philosophy for life is simply, "Eat the sausage while you can, for tomorrow it may be brown.")

Mr. Hillman, the lawyer in charge of Yelena's estate, called Joe Della Femina because he found an unpaid bill from Joe Della Femina Plumbing. He said he was sorry to inform him that Mrs. Helgit had passed away. Joe wasn't surprised, and the lawyer assured him that the bill would be paid. He also asked if Joe could come to his office, for Mrs. Helgit had left something for him in her will. Now Joe was surprised, and made an appointment for a couple of days later.

Mr. Hillman was the closest thing to a relative Yelena had. However, he had no intention of waking her body for a full two weeks in his own home (he lived in a studio apartment for the time being, as he was going through a divorce). Instead, he went ahead and had her cremated, to save on cemetery costs.

Her will was a complete shambles. Hillman had begged

her to get it in order, but the only thing that she was sure about was that she wanted to leave something to Joe Della Femina for all of his kindness. Mr. Hillman remembered Yelena's face when she would talk about the plumber, how it would light up the same as if she had just had a couple of Yanyaviks.

"It's her money," he thought, shaking his head. "She can leave it to whoever she wants."

nineteen

Todd and Missy were happy. It wasn't just the baby. It was Todd. He was different.

Missy had noticed that it all started with his new job at the Post Office. Todd's department head encouraged all of his employees to take advantage of the in-house psychiatrist available to all postal workers. After a certain amount of encouragement, prodding, cajoling, pressure and direct threats from upper management, Todd decided on his own to take advantage of the free therapy.

It was a brisk Autumn morning when he walked upstairs to Dr. Fellman's office, subconsciously resenting his boss for making him see a shrink. Todd's mouth was dry as he announced his name to the secretary, who, it seemed to Todd, was staring at him while stifling gales of laughter. Annoyed, he memorized the features in her face, in case he ever had to identify her in a lineup. Todd then turned and had a seat in the waiting area.

Twelve minutes later an older woman opened the door to the outer office and called his name.

She introduced herself as Dr. Fellman and extended her hand. She was sixty-two years old, heavy around the middle, and had snow white hair rolled into a French twist. Dr. Fellman wore thick, thick eyeglasses and had a sweet, grandmotherly face. She wore a beige dress, a white lambswool sweater and sensible shoes. Todd looked at her and felt instantly more at ease.

Dr. Fellman led him into her gray padded office, casually asking if he was currently on any medication.

"No."

"Would you like some coffee?"

"Yes, thank you," he answered.

"Well," began Dr. Fellman, cautiously, in an easy does it, put down your weapon tone of voice. "Why don't we start with how you're feeling about things in general. I understand that you're new to the Post Office."

"Have you heard something?"

Dr. Fellman smiled warmly. "I just wondered how you were doing as a new employee. I saw your lie detector test. I enjoyed it very much."

"You did?"

"Oh my, yes. You were obviously very honest. Let's face it, this wasn't exactly some breezy expense-account lunch interview—they really put the screws to you, but you did very well. I can tell you must be very strong, very confident to have come through it without breaking," she commented.

Todd didn't know how to respond. He was angry for having to be here. Come to think of it, he realized just then, he was usually angry. "Thank you," he said, finally, taking a sip from his styrofoam coffee cup.

"Tell me something, Todd," said Dr. Fellman. "I've told you one of my impressions of you. Could you share with me some of your own?"

"My impressions of myself?"

"That's right," she nodded.

"Why?"

"I'd like to know how you view yourself," said the doctor.

"Why?"

Dr. Fellman smiled to herself. Todd reminded her of her grandchild, Henry, the way he always asked "why?" "Because your inside world determines your outside world," she explained. "It's important, your self-opinion."

Todd had to think for a moment. Think hard. All of this was so foreign to him. He answered, "My mother always used to say that what was most important was her opinion of me. What do you think?"

I think you should come here every day for the rest of your life, thought Dr. Fellman.

"Todd, do you recall your very first memory?"

"Sure," he said. "I think I was about two years old. I remember that I was coughing and coughing and gasping for air and finally my mother finished her cigarette and I was happy because I could breathe again." Todd said this matter-of-factly, as if he were relaying that morning's weather report.

"And..." pushed Dr. Fellman.

"And what?"

"And do you have any anger attached to that first memory?"

"Anger?" Todd shot back, as if he had just caught Dr. Fellman trying to create a false memory in him.

"Yes, anger. Weren't you upset when you couldn't breathe, Todd?"

"No. I got used to it. It happened about twenty-five times a day."

"Do you ever get angry?" she asked him straight out.

"Look, I already answered that question on my job application," he retorted. "I printed it very clearly, right after my address and zip code. Yes, I get angry, okay? I'm a time-bomb ready to explode, so it's only natural that I'm a postal employee! Isn't that what you want me to say?"

Dr. Fellman didn't answer.

"There. You wanted me to get angry? I got angry. Now I'm a people pleaser, too," he said. "There's one more box you can put me in."

"Why is it so important that you don't get angry?"

"I don't believe in anger," he said.

"You don't believe in it? Or you're afraid of it?"

"What are you trying to get me to say? That I hate my mother? Big deal. Everyone hates my mother."

"How would you behave if you did believe in it?" asked Dr. Fellman.

"Believe in what?"

"You just said you didn't believe in anger," stated the doctor.

"So?"

"You've already admitted to harboring anger on your job application. Of course, why you'd confess to feelings of rage while seeking employment as a postal worker is, in itself, curious. Maybe," said Dr. Fellman, "maybe you wanted to get caught. Subconsciously, of course."

As Dr. Fellman spoke the last two sentences, Todd felt an alarm go off inside him. He realized that the woman in front of him wasn't just somebody's grandmother filling up her empty days. He knew that there was some insight in the things that she was saying.

"Todd, what I'd like to know, and what's really more important," Dr. Fellman continued, "is how you handle your rage. Would you like a cookie?"

Todd shook his head, although it was obvious to him that she had baked them herself. Oatmeal raisin. For a second he envied Dr. Fellman's children as they were growing up.

"How should I handle my rage?" Todd asked.

"I don't think you should," said Dr. Fellman.

"I don't understand, 'shouldn't handle it.' What do you mean?"

"I don't think anger should be handled. I think it should

be acknowledged and expressed."

"I can't," he replied.

"Can't what? Acknowledge or express?"

"I can't express it."

"Is that what you meant when you said you didn't believe in it? You meant you didn't believe in expressing it?"

"Yes."

"Why?"

"Because if I ever do let go…I…I don't…I'm afraid of what might happen." He searched Dr. Fellman's face, hopeful that she would know what he meant.

She did.

"You're afraid you'd lose control?" she asked, taking her knitting out of her sewing bag.

"Yes."

"So?"

"What do you mean, *so?*" asked Todd, beginning to lose control.

"I mean, what's so great about control?" she asked.

"It's the one reason that clerks, waitresses, policemen, people from all walks of life haven't killed my mother— they control themselves. If I ever give that up…"

"You'd kill your mother?"

They studied each other.

"Are you angry now?" asked Dr. Fellman.

"No. Why, do I look like I am?" asked Todd, chuckling.

"May I ask what's so funny?"

"Everything. This whole conversation is absurd, ridiculous, and, yes, laughable. Honestly, I'm probably the most well-adjusted man in the whole Post Office!"

"I agree."

"You agree?"

"Yes. But is that enough for you? Being the sanest employee in the Post Office, this is what you aspire to?"

"Well, it's better than nothing."

Dr. Fellman smiled. "Yes Todd, it's better than not being the sanest person in the Post Office."

Nobody said anything for a long time.

Todd watched Dr. Fellman, contentedly knitting away, straining to see the wool loops through her thick eyeglasses. It was nice here, he realized, just sitting, listening to the quick clicks of Dr. Fellman's knitting needles. He had never known anyone like her. She was sweet, yet direct and honest at the same time. Such an odd combination. Very rare, he decided. She made him feel safe, collected.

"Can I come back?"

"Only if you promise to tell me if I make you angry," she answered.

"Okay."

"Don't answer that so quickly. It's not that easy to tell someone you're mad at them, but we'll work on it."

twenty

Estelle was becoming more and more infatuated with, maybe even dependent on, the White Knight. His voice was with her all the time. He exhilarated her. She herself was confused as to why she was feeling this way about someone that she had never met. She thought about bringing it up at one of the Brave Women meetings, but decided against it. She didn't want to share him with anyone if she didn't have to. The White Knight was hers alone. Actually, he was all she had, since her husband had moved and Todd and Missy were becoming inseparable. "To hell with them," she often murmured in her sleep, as well as during waking hours. "I'll just get my own apartment and some cats. I definitely don't need to be around Missy's bad cooking and a crying baby. I've had my fill of smelly diapers, and I don't need anyone calling me grandma."

Estelle had tried calling the radio station to talk to the White Knight, but could not get through. She wished desperately that she knew where he lived so she could at least write to him, one sensitive soul sharing with another. There was only one option left now, if she wanted to find him.

twenty one

When Joe walked into Diane's apartment, she noticed that there was something mysterious about him.

"Hi," she said, searching his face for a clue.

"Hello yourself." And he kissed her.

"Something on your mind?" Diane asked, stepping back to get a better look at him.

"No, why?"

"You look funny, like something happened," she observed.

"Come here," he said, and again, kissed her.

Diane noticed even his kiss was a little off, like he was distracted, like he was simply going through the motions. Then they made love—talk about going through the motions! Joe, the person, was nowhere to be found.

While he was showering, Diane was making the bed. She grabbed Joe's pants, which were in a heap on the floor, and tossed them on the chair by the bed. A whole mess of change flew out and she picked it all up and stuck it back in his pants pocket. While her hand was in the pocket, she felt the unmistakable feel of a check. Diane debated back and forth for a good five seconds about whether or not to look. Finally, she took the check out and looked. It was made out to Joseph Della Femina from a law office—the check was for twenty-five thousand dollars!

Diane heard the water stop running and quickly put the check back. She was making the bed as Joe came out of the shower.

"So," said Diane, nonchalantly, "Come into any money lately?"

He stopped dressing. "You went through my pockets,

didn't you?"

"I did not go through your pockets, and where did you get that money?"

Surprisingly, Joe seemed eager now to discuss it with Diane, no longer angry that she had so obviously betrayed his trust.

"Believe it or not, you know that old lady I told you about, the foreign broad, the talker? You know, the one who liked to get smashed at lunch and yak about the old country?" he asked.

"Vaguely."

"Well," Joe smiled in disbelief, "she died and left me some money."

"Great! Now you can divorce your wife so we can get married. I'll call some caterers," said Diane, grabbing her copy of *Bride's* magazine on the way to the phone. "Which do you prefer, shrimp puffs or Swedish meatballs?"

Joe did not acknowledge either one.

Diane waited.

There was an awkward "Breakin' Up Is Hard To Do" kind of silence.

Diane felt tears coming on and blinked them away. Salt is terrible for the complexion.

Joe looked at Diane's reflection in the mirror so he wouldn't have to see her face to face. "I don't want to get married right now. Honestly, I..."

"This is it," thought Diane, "there's no kidding myself anymore. What a drag. I've hit a brick wall." Her entire life flashed before her eyes. It was the life of a single woman who never passed on her genes. A learned woman who died alone, unwrinkled and unloved. Someone who couldn't get past certain barriers, who could never exchange old feelings for new ones, who could never give up the comfort of a bad habit.

"Please," said Diane, "don't use that word, you only cheapen it—I don't mean that as an insult, really, it's just that for the first time I'm beginning to see the light in terms of..."

Joe interrupted. "In terms of me?"

"No. In terms of me," she said. "I think you'd better go." Listening to the door slam shut, knowing it was over, Diane felt empty. She picked up her *Bride's* magazine, went into the kitchen, and tossed it into the recycling bin.

twenty two

It was the beginning of the second week in October. Missy was now three months pregnant, and extremely nauseated. She felt better immediately, however, when she heard Estelle announce that she would be out of the house for a few days.

"I'm going into the hospital," Estelle informed Missy and Todd at dinner. They both looked up, concerned.

"Are you all right?" they asked simultaneously.

"I'm going to have some moles removed. It's an early birthday present to myself," said Estelle.

"Are you sure you wouldn't rather buy yourself a scarf or something?" asked Todd. "I thought you hated hospitals."

"That's just fear," said Estelle, "And I learned at my Brave Women meetings not to give in to fear. Isn't that right, Missy?"

Missy, much too nauseated from her pregnancy to contribute to the conversation, simply nodded in Estelle's direction. In fact, she did remember the topic being discussed at one of their meetings. Kyle was talking about being afraid to confront her boss. Diane talked about fear. She told the group what a real hero is. "A real hero," she said, "is not someone who doesn't admit she's afraid. A real hero is someone who says 'I'm not stupid, I know it's dangerous, but I'm gonna do it anyway.'"

Estelle continued. "So I thought the smart thing to do would be to make sure there aren't any problems. After all, early detection saves lives." Estelle smiled, revealing a set of yellow, smoke-stained teeth.

"Well," said Todd, "I have to applaud you. Preventative medical care is always rewarded."

"Yes," Estelle agreed. "It won't be bad—it'll be like going to a badly lit spa. If you're good, I'll bring you both something from the hospital gift shop. I've always maintained that you can't be too careful about your health." And with that she hurried out to the back yard for a cigarette.

Missy got stuck chauffeuring Estelle to St. Martina's hospital early the next morning, because Estelle pronounced herself "too weak drive." Missy stopped twice to throw up. Estelle offered some empathetic words. "I certainly hope your morning sickness goes away by the time you go into labor because mine didn't." Missy looked at her and threw up again.

When they got to the hospital the two women reported to the admitting desk. A nurse quickly got a wheelchair and sat Missy down, "You look awful. How long have you been like this?" she asked while signaling for an IV.

"She's always like that," said Estelle. "I'm the one checking in."

The nurse apologized and took the chair from Missy. She then reluctantly gave it to Estelle, who looked as healthy as an ox.

"Why are you here?" asked the nurse, skeptically. "You don't look sick. This is a place for sick people, people like her." She pointed to a semi-green Missy.

All the attention on her daughter-in-law infuriated Estelle, who was just looking for a little rest and relaxation (and the White Knight). "If Liz Taylor can check into a hospital at the drop of a hat, then so can I," she thought.

"I think that you should go home and rest, dear," offered Estelle, pushing a weak and dehydrated Missy toward the door.

"Wait. Let me give you something before you go," the

nurse insisted as she handed Missy something to help with her morning sickness.

"Oh, how nice," said Estelle, her patience growing thin. "I'll see you later."

Missy feebly stumbled out the hospital doors.

Estelle turned back to the administration nurse and asked, "Did I miss breakfast?"

twenty three

Diane thought a lot about life now, how hard it was, what it took just to get through a day. "Thank God for video rentals," she said aloud, and then remembered that that was how she met Joe.

It had been exactly three weeks since he left. She felt depressed from endlessly questioning herself as to whether or not she had made the right move by forcing the issue of marriage. She wondered if it was stupid to think that a person could *pretend* to have experienced a moment of enlightenment. "Or is it?" she wondered. "Maybe I did have one and I only thought I was pretending...what's the difference anyway? Either way the result is the same. What's the difference between pretending to have self-esteem and actually having it?"

One day a large box was delivered to Diane's house. She quickly got a pair of scissors and opened it. Inside, the box was filled with books—no, they were diaries—lots of them. Her first thought was that there had to be some mistake. But then, inside the box was a short note:

Dear Diane,
Along with the money the old broad left me her diaries. What do I want with somebody's diaries? Anyway, I know how you love to hear other people's problems

(that is your business),
so I thought maybe
you'd like 'em. If not,
toss 'em.
 Joe

Diane picked one up and opened it, noticing the date: nineteen twenty-five. Curious, she sat down and began to read.

Dear Diary,
Today when I was working at the Kebashnik fish factory one of the guards ordered me to put down the fish heads I was stuffing and come over to him. I hesitated, knowing that if I didn't stuff the required quota of fish heads for the day, by law I could be sent to prison. At first I pretended that I had fish guts in my eyes and did not see him. But he was persistent. Finally I went over to him and he led me outside, past the electric fence, past the rabid guard dogs, over to the lunch shed. There he told me to take off my hair net and gutting gloves and he reached down, found a spot on my face free from fish blood, and he kissed me!
Oh diary, I'm so scared. I wish he would leave me alone to do my day's work--I don't want to go to

*prison! I have heard these stories
about the guards from the other peasant
women, and now it has happened to
me. Who can save me? I know he has
a wife and she even works in the
underground part of the factory.
Please, I wish someone would save me.
I dream some day my prince will come.
Then he will be the one kissing me
and not some hunched-over guard with
ordinary fish breath.*

Diane put the diary down. "What a horrible life!"

twenty four

Estelle looked carefully around her hospital room. Was there any clue as to his whereabouts? Anything at all? Estelle could barely contain herself. Every male nurse that walked by intrigued her. Was he the one? Was he the White Knight?

A doctor came in the room and immediately told Estelle to put the cigarette out.

"But this is a private room," she argued.

"I don't care," said the doctor, shaking his head. "This is my hospital and you'll follow my rules or you'll get out." And with that he called a nurse and told her to give Estelle a catheter. When the nurse asked why, he replied, "Why not?" and left.

Estelle started to give him "why not" but stopped herself. This was too important. She couldn't afford to stand out. She would have to act like any other hospital patient. Just a run of the mill, ordinary woman. It would be difficult, she knew. Estelle had learned to live with her own extraordinariness. It hadn't been easy. It was her lot in life and she had accepted it, just like any other person born to greatness. It was who she was, which was fine for the everyday, but this situation did not call for the exceptional, intuitive woman that was Estelle Rogers. She needed to obtain information as unobtrusively as possible. If that meant keeping her mouth shut, so be it. Yes, she thought, that was her ticket to finding the White Knight, taking on the role of the passive patient. This would be her greatest challenge, she realized. Estelle had been saving passivity for death.

The nurse came toward her with the catheter.

•

Todd noticed his level of productivity at the Post Office had increased since he started seeing Dr. Fellman. His boss commented on it several times, which only served to increase Todd's newfound sense of self-esteem. Estelle didn't bother him quite so much anymore, though he dreamed of the day when he could strain his back helping her move into her own apartment. Todd realized that he was making so many discoveries about himself in therapy, so many discoveries about Estelle...

"Todd," said Dr. Fellman, "I'd like you to answer my next question as honestly as you can. Are you able to do that?"

"Of course, why do you even have to ask?" said Todd, the smile muscles in his face beginning to quiver.

"I'd also like you to stop smiling," said Dr. Fellman.

"Why?" asked Todd, his smile becoming even bigger.

"Because I've noticed that you tend to smile when you're nervous, and because I think you hide your pain behind that smile—not only do you not let your pain out—but you don't let the good feelings in. It works both ways: you don't feel your pain, but you also don't feel anything else. If you let the good feelings in, it'll feel really good," Dr. Fellman assured him.

All of this information was clearly overwhelming to Todd, and his smile began to subside. It was hard for him to let it go, like a child giving up his favorite blanket.

"What was the question you wanted to ask me?"

Dr. Fellman looked carefully at Todd and said, "Do you think Estelle was a good mother?"

Todd asked her to repeat the question—he didn't hear a thing after the word Estelle. The question was repeated.

Three times.

"*My* mother?" asked Todd.

"Yes."

"Well..." began Todd, squirming and cringing, obviously uncomfortable and flu-like. "...could you do me a favor?"

"If possible."

"In these sessions, could we make it a rule not to talk about my mother—ever—under any circumstance?" he asked, now entirely feverish.

"You want to do therapy and not talk about your mother?"

Todd sighed, obviously relieved.

"Yes."

"You've got to be kidding," said Dr. Fellman, putting down her current knitting project to scribble something in her notebook. When she finished she looked up at her favorite client. "Todd, does the word 'avoidance' mean anything to you?"

"That's a very becoming shade of lipstick you're wearing," said Todd.

"Don't make me repeat the question."

"The word avoidance means everything to me, I love that word."

Dr. Fellman sighed. "Todd, as you know, I'm quite a bit older than you. In fact, I'm probably about the same age as your mother. Do me a favor. I'd like you to think of me as your mother."

"That's easy. There isn't a woman walking the earth that I don't think of as my mother," Todd informed her.

"Okay, good," managed Dr. Fellman, hoping her concern for the young man didn't show. "What I want you to do for next week, is, think about confronting me, pretending I'm your mother. Okay? So don't forget, think about what you'd like to say." She smiled, "We had a good session today. Now then, I want you to go home and relax and I'll see you in one week." Dr. Fellman watched as Todd walked out of her office. "He's going to be one hell of a postal worker."

●

When Estelle woke up someone was speaking to her. It was a doctor. He shook her hand as he said, "The procedure went just fine. We'll know in two weeks whether or not you're pregnant."

twenty five

Missy was currently basking in the fact that Estelle was gone from her home. Even her debilitating morning sickness didn't seem so bad now. She felt free, relieved, exhilarated! Too bad Estelle was due back the day after tomorrow.

There was a Brave Women meeting that night and Missy was eager to attend without Estelle. She wasn't sure why, exactly—Missy just found herself looking forward to it all day. Finally she was sitting at the meeting, along with Carla, Judy, Kyle, and of course, Diane. Missy noticed that Diane was not her usual self. She seemed a little…sad.

"Who'd like to start?" asked Diane, her voice heavy.

No one said anything. Kyle and Judy studied the floor, Carla was off in her own mystery world, and Diane seemed preoccupied as well. Finally, Missy spoke up.

"I'd like to say something, if that's okay. I feel like I'm the only one in this room who's glad to be here." The others barely heard her, each was so caught up in her own problem. Or was there something she didn't know about? "What's the matter?"

"Our artificial insemination didn't work," said Judy. And with that she began to weep, at which point Kyle took out a plaid flannel handkerchief and handed it to Judy.

"I'm really sorry," said Missy.

"I guess I counted on it too much. I knew I shouldn't have gotten my hopes up," said Judy through her tears. "It's just that the donor was so perfect. He looked just like me."

"A dark, petite brunette," confirmed Kyle.

"It just didn't work." Judy started to cry again. Kyle held her as the group looked on sympathetically.

"Sometimes I think that life has its own timetable for

things," said Diane. "We shouldn't look at disappointments as disappointing. Maybe later we'll be really glad that things worked out this way. The important thing is to not let life's hardships destroy your relationship. I know things seem tough now, but look at it this way: you have each other. You're both young with your whole lives ahead of you. In other words, things could be a whole lot worse—you could be living in a country where they place more value on a fish head than on a woman's freedom."

"Diane, are you all right?" asked Missy.

"I'm perfectly fine. In fact, I'm better than all right. I'm...on my own for the first time in my life. I finally left a relationship that wasn't going anywhere. And I'll tell you, I feel as though I've had a complete facelift! It's wonderful."

"Then why are you crying?" asked Carla.

"I'm crying because tears are good for the soul—lousy for the complexion, but good for the soul. In fact, why don't we all just sit here and have a good cry, on me."

Everyone began to cry except for Missy, who had never felt less like crying in her whole life. She sat there looking at everyone sobbing and desperately wanted to join in, so she pictured Estelle coming home from the hospital and began to cry her eyes out.

●

Estelle saw the doctor leave the room and still could not make sense of things. What did he mean, "we'll know in two weeks if you're pregnant"? She buzzed over and over again for the nurse and waited. Finally a pretty young nurse came into the room. "What can I do for you?" she asked.

"What the hell is going on? Did something happen? I was scheduled to have some moles removed and the next thing I know I'm waking up and some doctor is telling me I might be pregnant!"

"That's happened to me before," said the pretty nurse, "once, after the hospital Christmas party. Let me go check with the head nurse and I'll be right back."

Estelle was fuming. What had they done to her? And where the hell was the White Knight?

twenty six

In her apartment, Diane was curled up on a chair watching the rain fall. Scattered on the floor were the volumes of diaries. In the bottom of the box they came in was a note from Yelena to a publisher. It read: "As I promise, here are my diaries all translated into English, perfect American English, like you ask. Now you read so you can publish, no?"

"So that's why all the diaries were in English. She must have died before any publisher saw them." Diane pieced it all together, happy to have something to do on a rainy day.

Dear Diary,
I am in prison now, because the guard would not let me alone to stuff my fish heads and I did not make my quota. The guard didn't care, he just found someone else to kiss in the lunch shed and did not even look at me as they put the brightly colored manacles on me and took me to the Kebashnik Prison.

The other women in the cell with me seem nice. There are twelve of us in all, but I am told that there are more coming.

Kebashnik has so many laws for women it's hard to keep them straight, so most women don't know when they are breaking a law. One prisoner told me that she was arrested because she was caught putting fish oil on her face to protect it from the cold. In Kebashnik, Plotzes are not allowed to engage in anything vain--it is considered a crime against the state. I feel so sorry for that woman--not only is she sure to be executed but she has such dry skin...

I have heard of a far away land called America. I knew a fellow commoner who went to this place and she soon sent me a picture of herself in America. I was amazed, because in the picture, this woman is wearing a hat! I could not believe it diary, because in Kebashnik a commoner is not allowed to wear a hat--and yet in the picture, there it is!

I could not help but wonder what kind of a land this America could be where a simple Plotz could wear a hat--in the daytime, even!

It is so cold in this prison cell that we cannot sleep at night. So the other night I woke up and heard much whispering--it seemed that all my cellmates were awake. They were sitting in a circle and all were sharing thoughts and feelings with one another. I asked to join in and they welcomed me openly. Pretty soon no one noticed the cold anymore and by the time we were finished, we all felt a little better about our situation. It was I who suggested that we do this same thing at least once a week in the middle of the night and even give ourselves a name. We chose to call ourselves Bravik Vamik (Brave Women).

Diane stared at the words. "Brave Women! Amazing," she mumbled, aware of just the slightest, briefest feeling of validation from what she had just read. "Maybe I'm not so untogether after all."

twenty seven

Estelle's stay in the hospital was nearing an end. As Missy was on the way to pick her up, she mourned for her loss and the hospital's gain. There was just a twinge of self-pity in Missy's thinking and she knew it. She decided to use her energy more productively. Instead of feeling sorry for herself, she decided to feel sorry for Judy and Kyle instead. She was so sad when they said that their artificial insemination didn't work. She wanted so much for Judy and Kyle to be successful in getting pregnant. She imagined the loving environment that they would provide for a child. She also imagined that she wouldn't feel nearly as guilty as she does now. "It's a very strange thing," she realized, "to look at some women and wonder who will be lucky and who won't." Missy counted herself as one of the lucky ones, but only briefly, only until she walked into Estelle's hospital room.

Estelle was still in bed. Missy was confused.

"Isn't today the day you come home?"

"You wouldn't believe what happened to me," cried Estelle.

Missy had never heard such panic in Estelle's voice before.

"What is it?"

"This damn hospital mixed up procedures on me— instead of removing a few suspicious-looking moles they confused me with another woman and they performed *in vitro* on me and removed some large freckles from her." Estelle lit up, daring anyone in that godforsaken place to challenge her.

Missy felt as if she were in a dream. "This can't be happening," she thought. "Now she'll never move out. No way am I gonna get stuck changing diapers with Estelle."

"Well, say something!" demanded Estelle.

"What am I supposed to say? That you can borrow my name book?" asked Missy.

"Sarcasm is not your strong suit."

"Look," assured Missy, "It's going to be all right—we both know it's not going to take." Missy thought that she detected just a hint of disappointment in Estelle's face.

"Well, what should I do?" asked Missy. "Shall I take you home?"

Just then the doctor walked into the room. "I understand there's been a little mix up."

"A little mix up!" said Estelle and Missy, simultaneously.

"St. Martina's is a hospital run by people, not computers. Once in a great while people do make mistakes, you know. Or are you perfect?" asked the indignant doctor.

Now Missy was really getting angry, but the old fears of looking foolish or unfeminine if she said something took over. She found herself thinking something she'd never dreamed of wishing before: *Why can't I be more like Estelle?* She envied her, sitting there puffing away, sizing the doctor up like he was a fly caught in her web, struggling to get out. She looked as if she were deciding when and where and how she would devour him. Estelle's power was definitely intimidating—and right now Missy admired it.

The doctor spoke nervously. "You know, it's not a good idea to smoke during pregnancy. And I've taken the liberty of writing out a prescription for some prenatal vitamins so you won't have to bother me—I mean, call me, later."

Estelle blew smoke in the doctor's face.

"Please, " he said. "I have asthma." He took in Estelle's

leathery face, saw the words "lawsuit" and "malpractice" written all over it and tried another tack. "I have an excellent tape for you to bring home. It's called *Welcome To The Wonderful World Of Motherhood*. Just in case you are pregnant, that is. If you're not, why, it'll make a nice shower gift for a niece or whomever..."

Estelle sat still in her hospital bed, waiting, watching, deciding.

The more she waited, the more nervous the doctor became, until he blurted out, "I'll take the baby! Just don't tell anyone. I'm up for chief administrator in a few months and I have a feeling this might hurt my chances. Please, you have no idea what it took for me to get through medical school—it was really hard! All those tests, memorizing all those Latin terms, touching a dead body the first day..."

"Shut up!" said Estelle.

"...and did it smell! Sorry." He looked down at his expensive shoes. "If it makes you feel any better, I think you'd make a wonderful mother."

Missy started to cough, then she started choking, then she couldn't breathe. Estelle and the doctor didn't even notice.

"You know, I don't say this to many patients, but you're still a vibrant woman, obviously in the prime of her life. If there is another life inside you…"

Estelle took another puff.

"…it'd be a shame not to let it breathe its first breaths in your arms." He smiled.

Estelle exhaled. Missy fought to remain conscious.

The doctor continued.

"I haven't known you very long, and I haven't spent a whole lot of time seeing you from this angle, but let me tell you, the pleasure is all mine. No, I mean it—you're really something, and believe me, I know. I've known lots of women, but none with your obvious sensitivity, your sense of forgiveness, your down-to-earth quality. I can tell you're a giver—am I right?"

Now Missy had to throw up. She ran to the bathroom, flung the door open and puked her guts out.

"I give till it hurts," confessed Estelle.

"I knew that!" screamed the doctor. "It's written all over your face. And what a face! Were you ever a dancer?"

Estelle tried to answer but was cut off.

"The reason I ask is because Isadora Duncan, the dancer, comes to mind so vividly when I look at you."

They stared at each other. Slowly, deliberately, Estelle took her cigarette and put it out in the red jello on her lunch tray.

"I'll need to see you in two weeks," he said, smiling.

"Yes doctor," whispered Estelle.

As he was halfway out the door, the doctor saw the present hospital administrator coming down the hall. He quickly turned back to Estelle and said, "You know, I have a hunch Freud was right when he said that there are no accidents." He then dashed out the door and ran for his life.

twenty eight

"Estelle, you are the worst mother in the world." CLICK. Todd turned off the tape recorder and turned to Dr. Fellman.

"Todd, why did you bring a tape recorded sentence to our therapy meeting? And whose voice was that?" she asked.

"My dry cleaner's," informed Todd.

Dr. Fellman observed her patient for a moment. "Now that you've clicked off the machine, do you feel better?"

"Yes, I'm glad I got it off my chest," he said. "I feel so relieved. It really helps to let your feelings out."

Oddly enough, he did look greatly relieved, which worried Dr. Fellman as she realized what a long way to go he had, and that's just what she jotted down in her notebook. "Todd, you realize you can't always talk through a tape recorder about things that bother you about your mother."

"Oh, God no, there aren't enough batteries in all the world!"

Dr. Fellman was relieved. "Good."

"I got a promotion at work!" announced Todd.

"That's wonderful."

"Guess what? I didn't even tell my mother," he added.

"I'm proud of you, Todd. You obviously didn't feel the need to win her praise, and it's unfortunate that, because you're not a psychiatrist, you have no idea how important that is. And I don't mean that to be in any way condescending, I just want you to know how happy that makes me. I approve—just kidding."

Todd didn't laugh at first but then the irony dawned on him and he giggled, a nice, hardy, from-the-gut giggle.

"I think that's the first time I've ever heard you laugh

honestly—boy is that nice!" noted Dr. Fellman, marking it down in her notebook. "I honestly feel that you're going to be just fine, Todd—in just a couple of years..."

Whatever was going on with Todd, Missy liked it. He seemed so much less nervous, so much more inclined toward enjoying life—his attitude regarding the coming baby, for example. He was so thrilled when she told him the news that he picked Missy up and twirled her, round and round. She had never seen him so happy. "It couldn't be just the baby," she thought nervously, and summoned the courage to ask him about it when he got home from work that night. She also decided not to tell him about Estelle and the hospital mix-up unless it was absolutely necessary.

As Estelle was checking herself out of the hospital, she looked everywhere and asked everyone about someone called the White Knight. Most people just stared at her as if she was crazy, slowly backing up and shaking their heads, anxious to get as far away from Estelle as they could, as quickly as they could. And since that was exactly how most people treated Estelle anyway, she didn't think anything of it. She was severely disappointed at not having met the White Knight, and she made a vow that she would never stop looking.

twenty nine

Diane was forced to reassess herself. She was no longer someone's mistress, no longer had a relationship to cling to and to define her. She would have to learn to do that all by herself. The prospect overwhelmed her. "Everything is designed for couples," she was realizing. "It's the whole Noah's Ark thing—everything's in twos, everything's a pair. Maybe I'll become a Mormon," she pondered, half seriously. Just then Diane realized something. Her thinking was all wrong. How could she have missed being half of a couple? She had never really been part of a couple—not in the traditional sense, at least. So really, in a way, she had lost nothing by breaking up with Joe. She sat, puzzled as to whether or not she should be comforted by this sudden discovery. The therapist in her felt justified, vindicated, but the lonely woman approaching forty did not. Finally, Diane snapped out of it, picked up Yelena's diary, and began to read.

> Dear Diary,
> Today the Kebashnik government was overthrown! They say that the new government is going to let all of us prisoners free just to spite the former regime. And now I don't know what to think. On the one hand, I am happy to know that after I am out, when I build a road or dig a swamp or put up a mile of fence, it will be for myself, not for the Kebashnik prison. But on the other hand, I have been in the Big House for two and a half

years. I won't say that I have grown to like the constant stench, the cot termites, and the fancy glassware—but I have a strange feeling that I might miss this place. I know I will miss my cellmates—all of them—as well as our midnight meetings.

I took pride in being a model prisoner—it was all I had. And now what will I be? Who will I be? The only comfort is that I know the other women must feel this way (at least I hope so). I will bring it up at our next Brave Women meeting which will be in two nights, on Wednesday, because that's the night they serve deep-fried fish heads for dinner, which gives all of us terrible gas and we can't sleep anyway—which is why we hold the meetings on those nights.

Diary, I want to confess something. Sometimes, when we are pouring the concrete for a new driveway for the warden's house, or some such routine prison task, I dream of becoming a writer! I know that I could be at least some sort of writer. If nothing else, I am confident that I could write many books informing people how to correctly put up a barbed-wire fence, or dig a trench, or get the rust off old iron bars. There are many things that I have learned here that I take pride in, that I know I am good at, and that is something I could write about. After all, I am only fifteen, and because I am so young, nothing out of the ordinary has happened to me yet. I know that with age comes experience and wisdom, so I guess I'll just dream about being a writer for now, and hope that I have an exciting life some day instead of the same old political prisoner routine.

Diane's eyes suddenly looked up from the worn pages of the diary. She could feel something awakening within her.

thirty

When Todd came home that night Estelle was in her room listening to the radio and leafing through a maternity clothes catalogue. Missy was setting the table.

"Hi," said Todd.

"Hi," said Missy, searching his face for anything that would explain the change in him.

"What's for dinner?" he asked.

Instead of replying, Missy took Todd's hand and led him to the living room couch. She hoped that the baby wasn't affected by the butterflies in her stomach.

"Todd, sit down. Please honey, I want to ask you something as long as we're alone."

He did as he was asked and Missy sat next to him.

"Todd, you seem so happy now...maybe happy isn't exactly the right word." Missy again studied his face and wondered what the right word was. "I think what I mean is, you appear...relieved, for some reason. That's it. I think that's it, anyway." She felt herself starting to disappear and struggled for visibility in her own mind. Why was she so nervous? He was her husband, she could ask him anything.

Nothing came.

"I think I know what you're trying to ask," he said. "I still love you. I promise."

Once again, he was her voice, he spoke for her when she couldn't speak for herself. Missy felt grateful and protected and guilty, the same chain of feelings she always encountered in her marriage. But she couldn't leave it there. She summoned the courage. She had to know more, even if she was afraid.

"Then what's going on with you? Why have you

changed so much? What brought this on?"

"Allergies—I'm kidding."

Now Missy was alarmed. Her husband never kidded, he never even laughed much. "Todd, what's going on? You're scaring me."

Todd looked away, in the direction of the staircase. After noting that Estelle was still upstairs, he turned back to Missy, took a deep breath and lowered his voice. "I really didn't want to say anything. I..." He stopped. Questions and doubts filled his mind. He felt awkward as to how to explain the source of his metamorphosis, the reason for his apparently noticeable state of relief. He decided that the best thing to do was to forge ahead and tell the truth.

"It's a new rule at the Post Office. All postal workers have to see a shrink as long as they're employees. It's so they don't snap or something, I don't know."

"You mean…you, and…therapy?"

"That's right."

He waited. For what, he didn't know. Maybe some kind of sign that she didn't think less of him. Missy's face revealed nothing. Frustrated, Todd made up his mind to stop searching female faces for approval, with the exception of Dr. Fellman's, of course. No, he decided, not even hers.

"It's the best thing that's ever happened to me."

"But Todd, you always said you hated talking about your feelings! You said it was dumb to get things off your chest, that it was right to keep bad feelings in, to let them fester and simmer and stew—that eventually they would go away."

Todd did remember. He was flattered that Missy had quoted him, but his own words now embarrassed him. He had never realized how afraid of his feelings he used to be. He sat, lost in his own thoughts for a moment.

"I did say that, didn't I? I'm telling you right now that I think that therapy is the best thing that I've ever done for myself and I regret that it took repeated threats from my boss to get me to go. Suddenly, it seems like anything in life is possible."

Missy sat silently next to her husband, confused. "I think I liked it better when I didn't know anything," she thought. "If everything is possible to Todd now, why would he settle for me?" She peered at his hands out of the corner of her eye. Todd was outrunning her. Her free weekly group therapy meetings now seemed pathetic in comparison to the emotional overhaul Todd was getting. Missy was sure that his therapist was going to point out all of her bad points, and there were so many of them. Of course Todd would see her differently. How could he not? She closed her eyes. Would he still love her? When she turned back to Todd he was staring at her. Something in his eyes was changed, she noticed.

"Do you still love me?" she managed.

"More each session." Todd took her face and gently put his lips against hers. "I'll never stop loving you."

thirty one

Diane stared at Yelena's diary and recalled that she, too, had once wanted to be a writer, when she was a little girl. Sitting there, it all came back to her. Memories she hadn't relived in years suddenly snuck up on her and demanded attention. Diane recalled a fifth grade composition of hers that the teacher thought enough of to read aloud. She actually remembered the excitement she felt after it was read to the class. The other kids going out of their way to be nice to her, treating her better than they had, like she was someone special. Diane shifted in her chair and gazed out her apartment window. Those childhood feelings were a great rush to the adult Diane. Her mind continued its backtrack, surprising her, exciting her. She recalled a forgotten passion for words that she held as a little girl. The sense of completion she encountered when she had placed two ordinary words side by side and saw the image they created, that *she* had created.

The limitlessness that this gift provided now made Diane feel powerful. It seemed strange that her dream had been so easily cast aside and forgotten. She wondered why. When did she let all of this go? It bothered her when she was neglectful, especially of herself. She certainly wasn't neglectful of the physical side. Why ignore a part that was seemingly much more potent, and certainly longer lasting than any physical beauty? "I had a *passion*," she realized. "If I hadn't given that up maybe I wouldn't have relied on men to make me feel important." Diane felt the anger start but decided not to waste any more time. Now just entertaining the notion of writing filled Diane with more purpose than she had experienced in years. "Maybe I could write a book…the thing is, I'm not sure that I have anything of value to say." Diane checked herself. She had made a promise to stop putting herself down internally. She rephrased the doubt. "Is what I have to say worth twenty-two fifty in hardcover?"

Her eyes wandered around the room and quite casually fell upon the picture of Joe Della Femina and his family at that amusement park. "I've got to get rid of this." She got up and took the photo out of the frame, and, because she could not bear to throw photos away, took out the old box that she kept for that sort of thing. "My God," she thought as she opened it, "there are dozens of old photographs of all my married lovers." And so there were. Twenty years of pictures of married men that she had known intimately. "Wow," she thought, looking at them, "men's ties used to be so wide." She took the entire box and poured all the photos onto her bedspread. "Why did I waste so much time on men who were married?" She tried to think of why it was that she was like this—not that Diane hadn't attempted to figure it out before—but this time she was determined to not only find out, but to stop the behavior entirely. Suddenly an image came to her mind from the diaries: *brightly colored manacles.* "I guess the modern day equivalent would be the image of a woman in stirrups. It's the time that a woman is at her most vulnerable," Diane noted. "That's always the time when I would seek out an affair—when I was most afraid," she realized. "If I can learn what triggers that fear, and then to get past that, in other words, to get beyond the stirrups, I could stop the destructive behavior." Diane stopped and smiled, "That's it. As I'm figuring it all out I'll put it down on paper so other women can learn from my mistakes! I'll call it *Beyond Stirrups: One Woman's Journey.*"

thirty two

Estelle was in the drugstore loading up on nicotine gum and patches when suddenly the thought of any form of tobacco repulsed her. "Odd," she thought, as the salesgirl put the items in a small bag. As she was walking back to her car Estelle looked forward to turning on the radio in the hope that the White Knight would phone in. Suddenly she was overcome by the greasy smells coming from the fast food place next door. "What's going on?" Suddenly Estelle's face turned white underneath all the makeup. "Oh my Lord…I couldn't be pregnant…could I?"

She ran back into the store to buy a pregnancy test, her mind racing. Frantic, she wondered if it could be true. In her suddenly frazzled condition, she thought about what everyone would think, about what the ladies at Brave Women would think.

Estelle and Missy had previously told the others at Brave Women what happened to Estelle in the hospital and they were appalled. It was Carla who seemed the most upset by the news, shaking her head and tsking for the rest of the evening. In fact she seemed barely able to concentrate on anything else.

When Estelle expressed outrage to the group that the pregnancy might take, each member thought privately there was no way in hell that life could actually begin in such a hostile environment.

Estelle was back in the parking lot, opening her car door. "I'll just have to forget about it until I take the damn test," she realized. She started the car and turned on the radio.

The voice on the radio came blaring out, startling Estelle. "And we're back!" it said, "We're of course speaking once again to the White Knight, who promised to tell us about the latest hospital screw-up. So, you were saying..."

"Yes," said the White Knight. "You won't believe it, but this woman, and I mean this woman around sixty years old came into the hospital—she just wanted some suspicious-looking moles removed."

"And?" asked the radio host, hoping to speed things up just a tad.

"And, the hospital got her mixed up with another woman who was having *in vitro* done."

"You can't mean that a sixtysomething woman may have been impregnated against her will?" asked the host.

"Yes! And what about the other woman? They removed twelve large freckles from her face!"

"Well, I can think of worse things…"

"Are you kidding? It turned out that the woman was part of a witness protection program! Those 'freckles' had been put there on purpose by the government. Now she may be recognized and killed before the trial even starts!"

"Plus, she's got fertility problems," added the sympathetic radio host.

"Exactly," confirmed the White Knight.

Estelle sat in her car, frozen. All sorts of feelings ran through her at this point—confusion, anxiety, flattery, nausea. She could not believe that the White Knight knew about her and what happened. How in the hell did he find out? She quickly came out of her deep thoughts so as not to miss anything being said on the radio.

"So you don't know yet if the pregnancy took?" asked the host.

"I'll know in half an hour!" shouted Estelle.

"No, I don't. I'll find out though, and I'll call again, I promise. This whole thing makes me sick. I feel sorry for both women. What if the pregnancy does take? What's this woman supposed to do? Can you take Geritol if you're pregnant? Going through labor could literally kill her. Plus, the baby is stuck with some doddering old woman as its mother. I don't think a woman in her seventies would make a good den mother for the Cub Scouts, do you?"

"No, I don't," said the radio host and Estelle simultaneously.

Estelle pressed the accelerator to the floor, eager to get home and take the pregnancy test to confirm what she already knew was true.

The radio host announced that, regrettably, they were out of time.

On the drive home she thought about how different it was to have a baby now as opposed to when she had Todd thirty-one years ago. "Missy's doctor said she can't smoke, can't drink, can't take aspirin, cold medicines, nothing. She told her she can't do or take anything! She can't sit behind a computer screen all day long, can't get a perm or color her hair, can't sit in the sauna..."

As Estelle pulled into the driveway she was still naming things that a pregnant woman in this day and age couldn't do. She quickly went into the house with her pregnancy test, announcing to all that she had to urinate immediately.

Five minutes later, a blood-curdling scream emanated from Estelle's bathroom.

●

Todd's sessions with Dr. Fellman were going well. Both were pleased at his progress. Todd had now learned how to verbalize his anger toward his mother, at least to himself, which was imperative, the doctor said.

Todd used Dr. Fellman as a surrogate so that he could release his feelings and let go of his anger. He no longer needed his tape recorder, and as his dark feelings began to dissipate they were replaced by excitement and anticipation about the baby he and Missy were having. His feelings about Estelle were still intense and difficult, but they were no longer deemed "dangerous to others" by Dr. Fellman.

thirty three

Diane had no idea how hard it was to write a book. Every time she sat down to begin she somehow wound up in front of the mirror experimenting with different skin hydrators. In two weeks she didn't get a single word written, but her complexion looked nice.

Finally, disgusted with herself, she picked up one of Yelena's diaries and began looking for something.

> Dear Diary,
> Today is my wedding day! I am so happy that I am scared something bad will happen. Two weeks ago my father told me that he sold me for two barrels of sausage. I am so proud--most of my friends from prison were sold for only one barrel! Can you imagine a man giving up all that sausage to have me as a wife? I can't believe it myself! My father tells me that he is an older man, a door to door herring salesman as well as a farmer, and thus will be a good provider. My father begged him to buy me and he did! In Kebashnik a female is not considered a real woman until a man chooses her for his wife. Please God, let me make this herring salesman a good wife. Help me to make my father proud of me because then I know I can be proud of myself. I have to stop writing now,

because before the wedding ceremony
can take place I have to serve the
sausage cups. I hope people like them--
I made them last night. **Well**, diary,
wish me luck--I will need it!

Diane kept looking at the page. She was wondering how
common laws and traditions affected women's self-esteem,
and how individual household mores altered women's self-
worth. "How did Yelena's environment affect her future?"
she pondered. "How did mine?"

thirty four

It was Sunday night, six days after Estelle had taken the pregnancy test. The Brave Women all settled down in their seats and waited for Diane to begin the meeting.

"Who'd like to…"

"Me!" shouted Estelle.

"That's fi…"

"I'm in a family way!" she announced, and then sat down and observed the faces before her.

"Oh my God," blurted Carla.

The others were silent. What had Estelle said? Could she have meant that she was pregnant?

"Could you mean that you're pregnant?" asked Kyle.

"Exactly," confirmed Estelle.

Missy was ashen. Carla sat tsking and shaking her head.

Diane immediately wondered how she could work this into her book. "It's incredible. It's like some kind of science fiction horror movie," she thought. *The Day The Earth Stood Still* was a title that briefly flashed through her mind.

Kyle and Judy were happy for Estelle but sad for themselves. Missy was just sad for the child.

"Well, what's wrong with everyone?" asked Estelle. "I was shocked too, but I'm getting very used to the idea."

"What do you want us to say?" asked Missy.

"Well, *congratulations* is a word that comes to mind," answered Estelle.

"How did this…I mean, don't you have to take hormones for this to work?" asked Judy.

"I was on hormone therapy for osteoporosis," said Estelle.

"Oh," said Judy.

There was quiet. *What does she want us to say?* they all wondered. Judy felt sure that Estelle's success would mean her failure. Missy thought of Todd, an only child for so long. Talk about having your kids far apart!

"You can't mean that you're happy about this, Estelle," said Carla. "I thought you'd be furious. Do you realize that you're going to be a grandmother and then a new mother within a few months of each other?"

Carla felt that someone had to point out some facts here. This whole thing was clearly overwhelming. While the others seemed to just sit there and accept this pregnancy as if the Pope were standing in the room with them, she would not.

"What's she supposed to do?" Judy asked Carla. "A glorious thing has taken place inside Estelle's body. I'm sure that hasn't happened in years."

The group stared at Judy. "What I meant was, it's been years since Estelle experienced being pregnant and it *is* cause for celebration." She turned to Estelle. "Congratulations. Besides," she added, shrugging her tiny shoulders, "it's already done."

"Thank you," said Estelle. "I know it sounds strange, but I am looking forward to it. At first I was furious."

"What changed your mind?" asked Diane.

Estelle answered, slowly, cautiously. "Well, I realized that if I have this baby, my biggest fear won't ever happen."

"What's that?" asked Kyle.

"I've always been afraid to live alone, but now I'll have the baby."

"You're seeing a baby as a companion in your old age!" said Diane. Her mind raced: *Oh my God, even bitter old wrinkled Estelle will have someone in her old age, and I won't.*

"So what?" said Estelle. "We'll travel together, I'll teach him all about art, and the finer things in life—a child could do a lot worse in this day and age."

"But that's too much to ask of a child," said Missy.

"How do you know? He might love it. I didn't seem to do too badly with Todd Junior, did I?"

It was all Missy could do not to blurt out Todd's true feelings toward Estelle. The urge was overwhelming, and it took every ounce of strength she had not to grab Estelle's padded shoulders and scream, "You're not going to suck the life out of another innocent child like you did with Todd!" Instead she looked away and mumbled something about "possibly sharing a diaper service".

At this point no one knew what to say, especially Diane.

"Are you going to sue the hospital?" asked Carla.

"No, I'm not."

Carla seemed genuinely disappointed and took up the rest of the meeting attempting to talk Estelle into taking part in an ugly lawsuit.

Estelle thanked Carla for her concern but suggested that she redirect her energy into throwing a fabulous baby shower for her.

Kyle and Judy exchanged a glance. They were both anxious to get home so they could privately devour this new information. "This may be the first concrete proof in history which confirms that even God makes mistakes," thought Kyle, guiltily.

Later, at the end of the meeting, Estelle could sense hostility from the other members as they gathered their things. It seemed to her that they were all giving her dirty looks. She didn't care. Since she had become pregnant she felt special, privileged, a success story amidst the current wave of infertility among young people. She felt young herself now.

Her body was doing what even Judy's and Kyle's bodies didn't seem to be able to do. It amazed and delighted her. She felt giddy. Estelle giddy isn't pretty, which may have accounted for the irritated glances in her direction from several members. Estelle couldn't get over the fact that not so long ago she felt achingly old. When her husband proposed retiring to Texas it brought to the surface a despondency she had experienced only once before, when her first baby was stillborn. Estelle did not want to feel that way ever again. She would not retire, would not live with old people—she didn't belong with them. She was young, she had always said it, and now even her body was saying it.

thirty five

Over the next month the non-pregnant members of Brave Women watched as Estelle and Missy grew heavier, bigger, and farther apart. Judy and Kyle tried to concentrate on their own lives and vowed not to let their infertility problems get the better of them. Since Estelle had announced her condition both women noticed an irrational dislike of her. When they were being completely honest with themselves, they had to admit that it was more than the rational dislike that any human felt for Estelle. Theirs stemmed from envy. Before, they had enjoyed certain aspects of Estelle's presence (after all, everyone has something to bring to the party, they both agreed), but now they found themselves avoiding her eyes, talking to her only when she approached them first.

"It's funny how pregnancy changes not only the woman, but the people around her as well," Kyle pointed out to Judy when they were exercising at their club one Saturday morning. Each assured the other that their troubled feelings did not show at the Brave Women meetings. Somehow, with Missy, Kyle didn't feel on the same awkward, unbalanced footing that she did with Estelle. She wasn't bothered by Missy's pregnancy. Kyle saw Missy as someone who was so grateful for what she had that she didn't, couldn't begrudge her anything.

But Judy did. Well, only in the smallest way possible. Judy allowed herself just the tiniest bit of resentment and then that was it—that was all, because she, too, liked Missy very much. Besides, there was a much bigger issue at stake than the predictable envy they were currently experiencing, and they both knew it. They were afraid that if neither one did become pregnant it would be their downfall as a couple. (Kyle had yet to confess her fear that Judy might go back to her husband, if only for the sperm alone. She knew she should say something, but for now she let it rest.)

During this time, Estelle listened in vain for the White Knight. He simply seemed to disappear from the air waves, and Estelle was convinced that he had met with foul play, which in turn filled her with an even more intense desire to know him. She listened to the radio all the time now, but not once did the White Knight make an appearance. In a way, she was frustrated, yet in another way she had grown attached to this clandestine need to comfort that she was harboring from the rest of the world. This voice had touched something soft inside her that nothing had touched in years, and in a way, a small way, it was enough.

Missy was now four months and three weeks pregnant, and her hormones had kicked into overdrive. She found herself crying most of the day, most days. Todd encouraged her to talk about her feelings the way Dr. Fellman encouraged him. Missy insisted through her tears that it was just hormones and it would pass. Todd wasn't convinced. He was worried about her. Nothing he did cheered her up. Finally he decided to let it go for now, because Dr. Fellman taught him that you can't help someone unless they want to be helped.

"How do you feel about your mother being pregnant again at her age?" asked Dr. Fellman.

Todd sat very still trying to gather up his thoughts. It wasn't easy to put feelings into words sometimes. "I feel sad because I know what's in store for that kid. I guess it would be like getting shot in the gut: it's awful, it's a long recovery period; but you finally heal, and then you read about someone else getting shot in the gut and you know what's in store for him."

"Try not to think in terms of clichés, Todd. I'm kidding. No, seriously, that's a very powerful analogy you laid out, it's a very strong image—but for now I'd like you to try to forget about guns and think about letting Estelle know exactly how you feel about things," said Dr. Fellman.

Todd swallowed hard. "Could I write my feelings and send them to her?"

"You can write a letter explaining your emotions toward her, sure," said Dr. Fellman.

"Well, I was thinking more like spelling out sentences using words cut out from magazines and then mailing the note anonymously," said Todd.

"Don't you think getting something like that in the mail would scare her?"

"How do you scare a bulldozer?" asked Todd honestly. "Nothing frightens that woman, I swear to God on my co-worker's lives."

"That's where you're wrong Todd," said the doctor. "Estelle is filled with fear, I assure you."

Todd stared at her, "There's no way in hell that I believe you—no way. How can you say that? You don't even know her."

"Not only can I say that but I'll go one better—you have now and have always had much more confidence than Estelle." Dr. Fellman waited patiently for Todd to fully absorb her words.

About fifteen minutes later Todd came to and said, "Answer me honestly—am I being experimented on?"

Dr. Fellman repeated her earlier statement and assured Todd that every word was true.

"How can someone like me have more confidence? My

mother doesn't care what people think! They can say anything to her and she's not affected—now me, if someone says they don't like my tie I'm ready to explode!"

Dr. Fellman wrote herself a note to warn Todd's coworkers. "Is that the reason you married a woman who doesn't like to confront? Because she's the opposite of your mother?"

"If I said yes that'd just make your day, wouldn't it?"

"I'm just pointing out the fact that your wife doesn't like to confront, whereas your mother…"

"Likes to confront," finished Todd.

"What I was going to say, was not that your mother likes to confront, it's that she likes to provoke. There's a big difference. I suspect that when Estelle provokes people, it makes her feel confident. Now do you still see her as confident?" asked Dr. Fellman.

Todd shifted in his seat. " I envy her because she doesn't feel bad. Ever."

"She doesn't let herself feel bad feelings, so she avoids a lot of pain. And you like this."

"Yes."

"Does a person who avoids things in life strike you as a particularly strong person?" asked the doctor.

Todd didn't respond.

Dr. Fellman went on, "What if a lawyer always wanted to be a judge? Suddenly he got appointed but he couldn't take the job because he was afraid to make decisions. He would avoid taking his dream job so he wouldn't have to face his fear, his fear of making decisions. Does that person sound very confident to you?"

"I'd rather be a lawyer than a judge anyway," Todd finally said.

Dr. Fellman waited.

"No," said Todd. "They sound more afraid than confident. Let me see if I understand, you think it's a sign of strength if a person feels hurt?"

"I think humans are designed to feel *all* their emotions: happiness, pain, love, sorrow, hurt—that's what they're there for. People get into trouble when they won't acknowledge certain feelings. Half the battle of removing a fear is to acknowledge that it's there. Find out why it's with you and you've all but conquered it."

"It's hard to admit that you're hurt."

"Yes," said Dr. Fellman, "It takes a lot of confidence, doesn't it?"

thirty six

Between work, Brave Women meetings and doing what she needed to do to get her book done, Diane had never been busier. And though she was sometimes extremely lonely, she noticed that at least her random moments of anxiety were less frequent.

Diane hadn't allowed herself to think about Joe Della Femina in months, until now. She found herself staring at a bottle of Liquid Plumr in her pantry, wondering how he was doing.

Diane's book, *Beyond Stirrups*, was coming slowly. Instead of the three hundred and fifty page book on self-esteem she imagined herself writing, the reality of the actual work involved was hitting pretty hard. Each week Diane rationalized a shorter and shorter book, until she realized it was in danger of being no longer than a *Victoria's Secret* catalogue.

She decided to join a Tuesday night writers' workshop at a nearby college. On the first night, Diane sat with the other students waiting for the teacher. Finally, a couple of minutes before the workshop was supposed to begin, the students could hear a loud humming coming from the hall. It started out low and gradually escalated and then suddenly stopped, just as most of the class was straining to name that tune.

A second later what must have been the source of the music walked in and wrote something on the chalk board.

"SURPRISE," he wrote, underlining each letter separately. Still silent, he turned to the class to watch them absorb what he had written. After a few seconds, the students, having read the word, wondered what it meant. The short, pasty, bald hummer simply continued to stand there, at the front of the room, watching them watch him. Soon the class began to move uncomfortably in their chairs. Diane felt a nebulous sense of embarrassment for the plump man holding the piece of chalk. She hated feeling embarrassed for people—it was one of those uncomfortable, runaway emotions that made her feel out of control.

Soon, people began whispering to each other. They were clearly ill-at-ease, some students beginning to feel hostile, not knowing what was expected of them. And yet the man at the front of the classroom continued to exude an air of calm, further provoking the students. The whispering grew more impatient. Still, he silently stayed put, smiling, taking large breaths, and eventually started to hum once again. This was almost too much, and the students began an angry dissent. Finally, the man-made music ceased, and for the first time actual verbiage emanated from his throat instead of a word-less showtune.

"Are you uncomfortable?" he asked the class.

No one attempted to answer. It was enough that he spoke.

"Did my behavior make you…uncomfortable? I would imagine it did," he said, looking at the class, though most would not return his eye contact. "But I'll bet it also intrigued you at the same time, didn't it?"

No one answered.

"I surprised you people with some out of the ordinary behavior and look what happened. You felt more in the last ten minutes than you have in weeks. You were embarrassed, angry, shocked, intrigued. What a wonderful glut of human emotion I instigated! As writers you should want no less for your readers. Do you see the power of catching your reader off guard? It's important, because writing without surprises is not writing, it is simply ink on a page and extremely…"

And he turned and wrote the word BORING.

Diane sat up straight while a few others shrugged their shoulders and shook their heads. She looked closely at the front of the room.

A girl in the front row raised her hand. "How do you surprise people when it seems like everything's been done? There's nothing new under the sun," she said. The other students agreed.

"Yes, I've read that before. It's true. Everything's been done," he said, shrugging. "Every plot's been thought of, every character's been described. You know what makes your writing new? You."

Once again most of the students looked to each other as if they had missed something.

"That's really all you've got as writers, your own unique response, it's your only weapon against the ordinary. If you can learn to tap into that part of you that is pure emotion without censoring it, and not be afraid of it, then you are limitless as writers. Uncensored emotion is as important to the writer as pen and paper."

Diane's hand wandered up to her hair and began to twirl it in an anxious rhythm.

"If you want to surprise your readers, sometimes you have to surprise yourself" he said.

A hand shot in the air. "What do you mean 'surprise yourself?'"

The teacher smiled at the flustered student. "I'm talking about allowing your most intimate feelings to surface, even if it makes you ill-at-ease, *especially* if it does, then we know you're not censoring yourself. If you can learn to do that, your own words will begin to surprise you."

They leaned a little closer to him.

"Right now I'm going to hand over to you lucky people

the sole secret to writing." He paused. "You may want to jot this down. The secret to writing," he continued, "is listening." The entire room looked up from their notes, puzzled. He hesitated, letting his students absorb his own personal theory on the subject. God he loved teaching! This was when he felt most alive, this was when he felt ageless, handsome, even, or at least not nearly as short. It was so thrilling to be able penetrate at least a few minds with collections of thoughts and beliefs that he had come up with. The teacher went on, his listeners curious. "When the artist sits down with pen to paper, or at the computer, he must allow his mind to be still, so that he can listen to his inner self. There is, in every writer, a pure voice that wants to be heard. Everything the writer needs is there for him—within his soul. All he has to do is hear it. That's what I mean when I say he must learn to tap into it. It's so simple a concept it may frighten some of you." He surveyed his students. "Some of you will know what I mean. The others will come to know what I mean, believe me. Anyone can write—all you have to do is let yourself. What I'm talking about is allowing yourselves to experience...you. The spiritual you, the real you. I do grade on a curve."

●

Estelle was in her room one night, leafing through a book of trendy baby names, when suddenly a familiar voice came over the radio. In the middle of considering Estelle Junior as a possible name, Estelle's concentration was snatched from her as she heard the words "tried to fire me from the hospital." Quickly, Estelle tried to focus. "It's him," she realized. It had been so long.

"Did you say the hospital did fire you?" asked the radio host.

"I said they tried, but they realized that they didn't have a leg to stand on legally, so then they tried to pay me to go quietly but I said no," answered the White Knight.

"Why now? Why did they try to fire you now?" asked the host.

Estelle nodded, eager to know also.

"I—well, they had another screw up, and believe me, it was a big one. It was..." He hesitated. "Remember when I told you about the older woman that the hospital accidentally performed *in vitro* on? Well, guess what? I learned some time ago that it took!"

"I don't understand. What did that have to do with..."

"I couldn't stand it anymore! This was the biggest mistake that they had ever made. They imposed a child on a woman, and she has to live with this mistake now for the rest of her life," he screamed. "I went to the head of the hospital and told him that I knew all about each and every screwup. I told him that I was the White Knight, that I was ready to stop hiding behind aliases and tell the whole world how this hospital made a soon to be sixty-four-year-old woman pregnant."

At the mention of what was obviously her case Estelle turned the volume up.

"I snapped," the White Knight continued. "That's when I told the hospital they either clean up their act or I'm going to write a tell-all book."

"What was it about this particular mistake that made you go to the wall?" asked the host.

Estelle sat, riveted. Now he was her White Knight, fighting her battles.

"This time it was different. This time it was personal."

thirty seven

The Brave Women watched as Estelle took her seat in the meeting, luminous in a vibrant green silk maternity pantsuit. "If Hugh Hefner was pregnant," thought Diane, "he'd probably be wearing exactly the same thing."

The ladies all privately wondered if that much light could hurt the fetus, but no one dared ask.

"Who'd like to start?" asked Diane, envying Carla's dark glasses.

Estelle raised her hand, letting more light into the room. "I have something that I've been waiting all week to bring up."

"By all means," answered Diane, finally putting away her writing assignment.

Estelle's eyes dropped to the acid-stained floor, as she felt self-conscious for the first time in her life. After dreaming of this moment for so long she found herself suddenly at a loss for words. She quickly hoped Missy didn't notice. They were all looking at her now, waiting, expectant, wondering. "I..." Estelle began and then stopped. Did she really want to do this? Did she really want to say this? To bring this all out in the open?

Suddenly there was another voice speaking, *the* voice.

Estelle looked up. She already knew who had interrupted her.

"I think this is something I need to do," said Carla, slowly, carefully. "I think it's time." She cracked her knuckles as the others looked on, curious. They watched as this previously familiar person became suddenly unknown. In an instant Carla stood up and removed a dark wig, sunglasses and a dress. Standing before them, clad only in shame and a pair of nylon gym shorts, was a five-foot-eleven-inch sandy-haired male.

The group gasped as they saw in front of them not a Brave Woman, but a man. He hung his head, revealing the beginnings of a small bald spot.

As fast as she could, Diane jotted something down in her notebook and then called everyone to order, even though no one had said a word yet.

No one knew what to say.

Finally, Diane broke the silence. "Why are you here?" she asked. "And why the ugly dress?"

"Oh, I liked it," said Kyle.

"I mean, what's all this about? Are you some kind of reporter?" Diane pressed.

"Hardly," said Estelle.

"Then what are you?" asked the rest of the group.

The White Knight slowly lifted his head, cautiously avoiding eye contact, and began to explain. "As you already know, I'm a man. The reason that I dressed up like a woman is because I knew you wouldn't let me be a part of this if you knew I was a man. I needed a place where people talked about the things that bother them."

"So why us? I mean, I'm reading all the time about the men's movement," Diane said, rolling her eyes. "Why didn't you join one of those groups? I think I just read about a new men's group called the Arrow Heads—I think it's in the suburbs someplace."

"Yeah, why didn't you join their club and pretend to be a man?" asked Kyle, who immediately wished she hadn't. "Sorry," she said. "I guess I just feel really betrayed."

"It's okay, Kyle, I deserved that. Let me start by telling you my real name."

Estelle looked him in the eyes as he spoke.

"My name is Allan and I'm a male nurse." He waited for the inevitable giggles; there were none. That touched him. He turned to Diane. "You know the question you just asked? Well, you kind of answered it yourself. What I mean is, there are all sorts of new men's groups popping up all over, you're right. But that's the point—they're new. Men are still just taking baby steps in this area, whereas women have been doing this for years and years."

Diane thought of Yelena's diary and found that she could not argue.

Allan continued. "I did go to one men's group. They're relatively new, about six months old, they call themselves the Indian Givers. Don't get me wrong, they're a perfectly nice group of men. It's not that they don't talk—they do. It's just that the conversations always ends up being so…surface, if that's the right word." Allan looked around, anxious to see if he was making any progress with his all-female jury. He wasn't. Fumbling, embarrassed, not to mention chilly, standing in only his gym shorts amidst the icy stares. "That group didn't generate the warmth that I enjoy here with all of you," he bleated.

The women sat staring at Allan, unblinking, not knowing what to say, or what to feel. There was a long, painful silence, fueled by an enormous, unanimous hurt felt by most of the real females in the group.

Diane was most humiliated. She was the leader of the group, the one the others looked up to, and she felt that she had let them down. "How in God's name could he have fooled me?" she asked herself. "Hell, I actually sat here some evenings wondering what kind of night cream Carla used." Diane addressed the group. "I feel so duped, so taken advantage of…"

Everyone but Estelle nodded.

Kyle spoke. "I feel like all my fears, prejudices, and free-floating anxieties about men are justified now."

"So in a way this must be a little gratifying for you, Kyle," noted Diane.

"In a way."

Diane herself experienced a small amount of relief, for, though she never realized it until now, she secretly feared that Carla was really Joe Della Femina's wife seeking out some kind of revenge.

Judy, holding tight to Kyle's hand, said, "I've been sitting here, trying to remember all the things I've said to all of you in what I thought was the privacy of a women's group."

"Me too," said Missy.

"If everyone else jumped off a bridge I suppose you would too," said Estelle quickly.

Missy, suddenly enraged at Estelle for pronouncing her reaction nothing more than a copy-cat one, fired back. "No, Estelle, that is the way I feel. Judy just happened to put it into words first—so glue that to your forearm and smoke it!"

Everyone in the room, including Carla gasped. They had never heard Missy address her mother-in-law like that before. What had this man done to their group?

"Look," said Judy, "the thing that I realized is that I don't care what I've said. In fact, I kind of feel a certain freedom. Now I feel like I can say anything I want to a man because I've already done it! You don't know it, but I grew up being told that a woman's place is wherever her husband wants her to be." She looked lovingly at her partner. "And I don't feel that way with Kyle."

"So in other words, you feel like you've conquered one of your biggest fears," said Diane.

"Oh yes, I can think of so many things that we've talked

about here, that *I've* talked about that I know I could never have uttered in front of anyone male. And now, not only do I not care, but there are so many more things I feel like I can say—I just love it! It's just such a relief to me," said Judy. Swept up in a wave of mutual understanding, Missy jumped in, eager to share her feelings.

"I know what you mean. Remember in high school, when a guy said that he might 'stop by' that night? And you had to spend the whole evening just 'casually' sitting around wearing your best outfit, your hair curled, and all your makeup on, in case he did just 'happen' to stop by?"

Everyone, including Allan, nodded bitterly.

"Well, now I feel like I've been seen without my make-up on, so to speak, and it didn't kill me. It kinda feels good," continued Missy.

"Well," said Diane, "those feelings are nice and I'm sure that we've all benefited somewhat by being duped. But we still have a problem: Allan is not a Brave Woman."

"I think he's a brave *man*," interrupted Estelle.

"That's a matter of opinion," said Diane. "The question is: does this brave person stay?"

"I think Allan should stay," said Estelle quickly. "After all, he's proven how sensitive he is, and since Judy obvious-ly didn't mean it when she claimed she was going to med-ical school, it'd be nice to have a trained health-care profes-sional on the premises. I don't have to remind you that I'm empathizing for two now, and with the rising cost of doc-tor's visits I know I'd appreciate a little free medical advice now and then."

Judy stood up and ran from the room, fumbling for the keys to her car.

"Well," said Diane. "Would anyone else like to go?" Everyone but Estelle stood up and began gathering their things.

As Allan got dressed he felt the eyes of the group on him. He looked up at Estelle as the others frigidly packed up their belongings and filed out in a huff. Allan regarded Estelle lovingly, grateful for her thoughtfulness. He smiled and she flashed him her own lipsticked grin. In that instant, the two became friends, and felt an immediate sense of camaraderie.

thirty eight

Diane sat in the workshop, nervously waiting for the teacher to give back their first assignments. Larry, as his students called him, asked that the compositions be "anything you feel strongly about. Anything—a person, an inanimate object, a wonderful meal—whatever. Just make sure that what I see on the page are not words, but feelings. Tell me things I've never heard before."

Diane felt someone tap her on the shoulder. She turned around as Larry was handing her composition back with a grave look on his face. She quickly took it and read the comments at the top of the page.

> Miss Turner:
> Obviously feelings and emotions are not anything you deal with very often. Most people, when writing about the day they learned that they had been falsely diagnosed with cancer, would be able to communicate something of what they felt. Here you have a subject matter which most people have never and will never even begin to fathom, and yet you managed to make it dull. Why include boring details like what the oncologist was wearing beneath her white smock? I honestly

don't care if her eyebrows were thin, and I would imagine you were feeling a lot more than you have the guts to admit. Maybe it's just me, but I really don't care to know who dedicated that wing to the hospital in 1928. There is a distracting shallowness to your writing. Put another way, your work is all surface. Are you aware of this? Next time, don't be afraid to expose yourself to your reader.

Diane stared at his comments, devastated, her whole body hollow. "Do I do that in real life? Do I distract myself with ongoing projects involving my physical appearance? Yes, maybe." In her mind, suddenly quieted by the rejection, she heard the words *write down how you feel.*

Blindly, she did. So overwhelmed by the stunning setback, Diane's mind was partially blank, shell-shocked, uncluttered, allowing her deepest thoughts to surface without interruption.

After she finished, Diane opened Yelena's diary (she had taken to bringing one with her wherever she went, like an engaging paperback) to compare the two writings. As she read, things began to clarify in her mind. Diane was starting to see what Larry meant about surprising yourself.

Back at the front of the room, the teacher addressed his students. "For next week's assignment," announced Larry, "I'd like everyone to write about an inanimate object. Something we see every day."

A good-looking man with a calculated five o'clock shadow and a tweed sport coat raised his hand. "How do I write passionately about a washing machine?"

Larry smiled. "How do you write passionately about a beautiful woman?" he proposed, staring openly at Diane. The rest of the class followed their teacher's gaze, turning their heads, curious as to whom he was so unabashedly looking at.

Taken by surprise at the sudden spotlight thrust upon her, Diane swallowed and averted her eyes. She could feel his stare, his interest, his intensity resonating all the way to the back of the room, where she was sitting. She felt disoriented. It was not that she didn't like attention paid to her, she did. Why else would she endure years and years of self-sculpting, dieting and odorous hair dyes? Yes, she liked attention from men, loved it, even lived for it—but Diane liked attention on her terms.

The teacher continued.

"Listen and the passion will come. Learn to trust yourselves. Listen to your inner voice and let go. Like I said before, a good writer is often surprised by what he has just written. That means that he didn't analyze and didn't get in the way of the words. This brings us to another essential element in writing: honesty."

Diane instantly looked back up at the mention of the word honesty. Her stomach clenched. Diane had trouble being honest with herself, and, as much as she could truthfully admit to herself, knew it. She thought back to her teacher's words the first day of class: "The secret to writing is listening…to the real you."

"The real me," she pondered. "I don't know if I can do that." She sighed, aware now of an unexpected barrier that could prevent her from pursuing the writing. It was something she'd have to seriously consider, letting the real Diane come out on paper. Revealing herself in black and white. It was scary, although it had been a long time since she reflected on something so carefully. Diane noted curiously that she had had years of therapy, but for some reason the significance of self-honesty had never seized her in quite this way before.

The bell rang and she quickly gathered her things. She could feel her teacher looking at her again and it made her uneasy. Actually, Diane could not decide which feeling he evoked in her; did he bother or excite her? "I know I'm not physically attracted to him—probably because he's not physically attractive." She closed her notebook and hurried out of the classroom. She did not want to give Larry a chance to talk to her. His openness troubled her.

From behind his desk, Larry watched as his attractive student gathered her things and rushed out the door. He knew she didn't like him.

He was used to it. Women never thought of him like that. He was a prisoner of his appearance, but then most people were. He could think of worse things.

Larry walked over to where Diane had been sitting and noticed that she had forgotten something. He bent down and picked it up. It seemed to be a diary of some sort.

Larry looked closely at the forgotten diary. Ethically, he knew he shouldn't read it, but in every other way he was dying to know what secret thoughts, desires, and current boyfriends Miss Turner was harboring. "It's probably as close to her as I'll ever get" he realized. Even so, he reluctantly decided not to read it. "I'll just take it home and give it to her in class next week," he told himself, putting it in his briefcase.

He walked into his apartment that night after class and turned on the lamp next to the couch. He set the briefcase down, removed his coat, and went to fix himself a vodka tonic. With drink in hand and the best of intentions, he settled in on the couch in his cozy living room, determined that he was capable of out-wrestling any and all curiosity. Larry sipped his drink and thought of his day, all the while knowing, that he had no interest whatsoever in reviewing his day.

He eyed the briefcase. It was quiet in the apartment, the only sounds were the ice breaking in Larry's vodka tonic and the ticking of the antique clock above the fireplace. Time sauntered by, taunting him, seemingly aware of his suffering, a victim of his own blatant nosiness. Finally, he broke, and rationalized that on some level Diane must want him to read the diary, otherwise she wouldn't have left it behind. "The subconscious is powerful," he remembered having read in *Psychology Today* while waiting for his car to be repaired. Actually, Larry pooh-poohed the idea until now.

Now he realized how much it seemed to make sense, and how it was as good a reason as any. He finished his vodka tonic, took the diary out, opened it to a random page, and began reading.

> Dear Diary,
> I am all alone now. My husband has died. It was a heart attack. He was in the barn milking our cow when suddenly, with no warning, the cow had a heart attack and fell on my husband and killed him. Fortunately the cow lived, and I was able to sell her to pay for my husband's casket. Now what

am I going to do? I am all alone, my family has all moved to Estonia for the mild winters, and unfortunately I have heard that some of my old cell mates were sent back to prison by their husbands. A few were even executed because of poor attitudes. Oh, diary, I don't mean to complain, but now what? The winters here are so cold and the summers only last a week. That's why we have the Paprika Festival, to celebrate summer because we're so grateful for even a little warmth. That's also why our greatest Kebashnik delicacy is called summer sausage. Now I have no husband, no house, and no cow. My only hope is that another man will want to buy me. But the chances of that seem slim.

"What's going on?" Larry asked himself. "Could Diane be putting me on? Is this a joke? That's probably it," he thought. Larry kept feeding his paranoia, imagining Diane somewhere laughing at him. He fixed another drink, and found he was drawn back to the diary like a magnet. He finally gave in and settled on the couch and read the entire thing.

It was now three o'clock in the morning, and in the time he had spent reading the diary he felt as if his mind had been on vacation, been somewhere else, while a different part of him took over. A part of him that was unspoiled and child-like, a part of him that didn't get out too often.

As he was reading, the words seemed to be reaching out to him in a personal way. That was the height of the literary experience, Larry had always maintained: an intimate connection with the reader. And that link could only come through an uncensored voice. The written word was the most underestimated force in the world, he felt. It was the way humans connected.

He sat on the couch, his whole body littered with uncommon feelings. The woman in the diary was real to him. Maybe she *was* alive and living in the imagination of Diane Turner.

thirty nine

Allan had always wanted to help sick people. Ever since he could remember, he had felt an affinity with those who were ailing. For most of his youth, he believed that he himself was sickly, but it turned out that his mother was a hypochondriac once removed: she herself was never ill, but constantly imagined that he was. This left him with an empathetic ache in his heart for those who were sick. Aiding ill men and women was only a beginning for Allan. He quickly discovered after becoming a nurse that he could not bear the thought of any kind of medical mishap on an innocent patient, for when he witnessed such an occurrence he re-lived his mother's neurotic impositions on his own childhood. He had an unquenchable desire to right the wrongs of the medical world.

Allan spent his youth in front of the television, mesmerized by hospital drama shows. Fascinated, he was able to absorb so much medical information that later on nursing school was a breeze. Allan decided against becoming a doctor because he noticed that on all these television shows the unsung hero was always the nurse.

"It's the doctors who hand out the prescriptions, but it's the nurses who hand out the compassion," he told his graduating class from nurse's college. He graduated with honors, though it took him six years to get through the program because he had to work a full time job as a short-order cook to pay for tuition (Allan would not take a penny from his mother after she imposed her hypochondria on him his whole childhood).

Allan's own theory was that his mother kept insisting that Allan didn't feel good so that she could keep him home from school to keep her company. She was lonely after Allan's father left her for a younger, healthier woman. Allan also suspected that this was her way of going about trying to meet an attractive doctor. "I was a child pimp," he often thought, still bitter. In fact, his resentment toward her knew no end, it seemed. Even though he had said his good-byes years ago, refusing to see her, she continued to haunt his daily thoughts. Allan knew that he might just as well have continued having a relationship with his mother, for all the time he spent with her in his mind. Then at least he could have gotten something out of it, perhaps a free meal on Sundays or cash on his birthday. Allan just couldn't let her go, even though he still felt hurt by her. In a way he knew he was punishing himself but could not help it. He realized that he should see someone to resolve this issue, but since he was working his way through nursing school and money was tight right now, he'd just have to settle for afternoon talk shows for therapy. They helped for a while, but he wisely recognized that he needed more.

Allan noticed that when he had conflicts in his life they usually involved women. He was never sure if he created the negative incidents, or if it was just a coincidence that female relationships ended badly for him. Allan knew that he had a tendency to place women on pedestals. He was both infatuated with and terrified by the opposite sex. Some of his romantic partners accused him of an inability to fully commit to the relationship. The women usually said the same thing: they felt that there was a part of Allan that didn't love them. He did all the right things, they said, in fact he was more than affectionate, generous and giving. It's just that when it came right down to it, Allan held back a part of himself, and that translated into a feeling of inadequacy for his partners.

It was his friend Carol who suggested that he become a haircutter for a while if he truly wanted women to confide in him and let loose with their thoughts and honest feelings. Perhaps observing them in this setting could help. Allan declined, sensing that this was just a quick fix, and knowing that realistically, he had absolutely no talent for cutting hair. He decided that he needed to get to know that part of himself that he was afraid to reveal to women. One thing that he knew was this: if he could somehow get inside the minds of women, they would cease to terrify him. It was, he was sure, the key to becoming what he was not yet fully, but had always dreamed of being: a real man.

●

The members of Brave Women were just getting seated when Allan walked in, dressed, this time, as a man. There was a chilly silence throughout the room as he made his way to his chair, next to Estelle, the only welcoming face.

"Okay," said Diane, "does any-"

Allan stood. "Could I...could I please say something? Would that be all right? I just really want to get some things off my chest."

"You mean you want to talk about yourself Car- I mean, Allan?" asked Judy.

"I would love to, if I may?" he looked around, eager to find one nodding head besides Estelle's. There were none.

Finally, Diane spoke. "First of all, Allan, you don't have to stand. Please." She motioned for him to sit, which he did. "Secondly, if you want to share, well I guess there's no stopping you, is there?"

"Thank you Diane," Allan said earnestly. "I appreciate the chance." He began to look at the faces before him, but quickly turned his vision elsewhere. They frightened him, but this was something he had to do. He had made a promise to himself earlier that he would not, under any circumstances, cry.

"First, I'd like to say that last week, I told you something that was only partially true."

"So what else is new?" asked Diane.

"When I said that the reason I wanted to be in a women's group as opposed to a men's group was because ladies are better at talking about their feelings than we are. I think that I said you were better at it, because you've been doing it longer."

"That is what you said," remembered Diane.

"Well," said Allan, "what I want to say, and what I've never admitted to anyone else in my life..." He paused, remembering his promise to himself not to shed tears. "...is that I am, and always have been, haunted and obsessed with women."

"So am I," said Kyle. "What's the big deal?"

"No, no," said Allan, suddenly unafraid. "Please don't confuse perfectly normal homosexuality with the unconscious bondage I feel toward the fair sex."

The whole half-W sat up straight.

"I knew I always loved women, but slowly I realized that what I felt for them was also something different. I realized that I seemed to be confusing love with what a book termed 'erotic spiritual power.'" The room was still as Allan filled the air with groups of words the ladies had never heard before. Erotic spiritual power?

"See, in my mind, women have always harbored a power," Allan continued. "It's my own personal theory that on some level all men are in total awe of women."

I agree with that, thought the group, nodding.

Diane spoke. "I still don't understand why you wanted

to belong to a women's group."

Allan searched carefully for the right words. "Someone once said that the way to truly become a man is to come to terms with the fact that men idolize women. But it's really not live, flesh-and-bone women—it's the image we carry around in our heads that we hold in such reverence. This awe we feel is threatening to us. So we tend to react inappropriately. I, for example, tend to pull away. You have no idea how much men are enmeshed, inwombed, and defined by women."

"How come you can't get 'em to marry you?" asked a cynical Diane.

Allan laughed.

"Seriously, though," Diane resumed, "that just doesn't make sense. My father constantly pushed my mom around."

"Ahh," said Allan. "I'm glad you brought that up. Let me ask something here. Did anyone ever stop to wonder why it's always men who are the rapists and the killers?"

"Women are starting to break into those areas," said Kyle, defensively.

"Okay," Allan, acceded, "But why is it almost always men who stalk and hunt for the sole purpose of raping and then killing women?"

"They're afraid to commit?" asked Diane.

"No, they refuse to admit the power women have. They fear, therefore deny, therefore try to control, through rape and murder, the power of women," Allan insisted. "At least, that's what the guy on the infomercial said."

"Wait a second," said Diane, "you're saying that some men hate women and rape them because they are threatened by our power?"

"Yes," answered Allan.

"Last time I looked it was a man's world," said Kyle.

"Men have all the power."

"That misconception is what men are fighting so hard to maintain—some think it's worth raping and killing for," Allan replied. He drove his point home. "If men weren't so threatened by women, why would we spend so much energy trying to control, conquer or demean them?"

"Habit?" offered Kyle.

"I always thought it was the opposite. I thought some men dominated because they could, because they were confident," said Judy.

"If you're confident, you don't have anything to prove," said Diane, in a new moment of recognition. She thought quickly of Joe, how he always had to subtly put her down. She felt a giddy sense of justification in the fact that she had initiated their split-up.

Allan continued. "I was reading a book about how to be a real man, called *How To Be A Real Man*, by Dr. Scott Biden, MD, and it helped me enormously. It said that the best way for men to rid themselves of this unreal image of the opposite sex in our heads is to dispel false mystification, see women as they really are: ordinary human beings who just happen to be the ones that God chose to give the ability to bring new lives into the world," Allan said, looking at Missy and Estelle as if they had the Shroud of Turin draped across their stomachs.

"I think you still need to work on the demystifying thing," said Diane. "But there's no need to go too far," she cautioned.

"Is that why you chose a women's profession, like nursing? Because you wanted to be around women?" asked Kyle.

"A *mostly* women's profession," said Allan. "Subconsciously, maybe. I think I was just fascinated by your sex."

"Didn't working with females help to demystify them for you?" asked Kyle." I mean, why did you still feel the need to join our group? Wasn't that overkill?"

"It wasn't the same because I experienced those women as a man, not as a fellow woman like I did here. If you think that there isn't any difference in the way we treat each other, you're wrong. I pretended to be a woman to attempt to see women as just ordinary people, with ordinary faults."

"And did masquerading as a woman allow you to see us as ordinary people with ordinary faults?" asked Kyle.

Allan stopped for a moment, realizing that he hadn't even asked himself that question since joining the group. "I...I see that women have their share of struggles, are confused at times, but in a sense," Allan sighed, resignedly, "in a sense, I'm much more in awe than I was before."

There was an audible gasp in the room. Each woman was stunned to learn that after having been observed delving into their most private pain, that they emerged...*desirable*.

"Wow. You're much more of a man than I thought. I mean, I guess I just assumed that all male nurses were gay," said Judy.

"You know," replied Allan, "it's really funny, but now I realize that all my life I've lived in fear of being labeled a sissy, a wimp, of not being a macho man."

"And you thought being a male nurse would help?" asked Diane, immediately sorry for making the thoughtless joke. "I'm sorry, Allan."

"No, it's okay. It's not you, it's the way we're brought up. Seriously, I wanted to become a nurse because they are the ones who are really around the patients. They are the ones who get close, and I don't care what kind of man it makes me. You're not the first one to make a joke. I know about discrimination, for God's sake—I'm a MALE NURSE! People don't think that I can hear the snickers and the giggling behind my back. I just wish some of you could have been there the day I went in to buy my regulation white nurse's shoes..." He stopped, too upset to continue.

By this time, there wasn't a dry eye in the house, including Diane's.

Allan regained his composure. "Why are male nurses considered fair game? Why is it considered better for a man to be a beer drinking, overweight construction worker who yells obscene things at women than to be a male nurse?"

"I don't know, but it is," admitted Diane.

"I'm sure that construction worker doesn't have trouble getting dates, like I do. The minute I tell a woman I'm a male nurse, she's turned off—I can see it in her face." Allan paused, as if making up his mind whether or not to continue. "Okay, let me just say one more thing and then I'll shut up: I thought that if I wanted to become a real man, the only way to do that was to learn to love and respect women as they really are. Then I could let go of that overbearing image of them I carry in my mind. In order to become a brave man, I first had to become a brave woman."

The ladies were, by this point, beside themselves. There was no question that they all wanted him to stay—also, most were racking their brains, trying to think of a cousin or friend of a friend to fix him up with. Definitely a woman who could appreciate someone as unique and sensitive and honest as Allan.

forty

Missy was five months and three weeks pregnant now, and she and Todd were really starting to get excited. Todd seemed to get promotion after promotion at his job, which he largely credited to Dr. Fellman. Todd also encouraged Missy to speak up for herself.

"Dr. Fellman said it's not good to hold things inside."

"Shut up!" said Missy.

They were both stunned. This was the first time in their marriage that she had dared to spout such a demand. After a silence, Missy blurted out, "I'm sorry, but all you ever talk about is Dr. Fellman. I'm sick of hearing about her." She turned from her husband, the first person in her whole life that she had ever told to shut up. She didn't mean to, but he was just driving her crazy with second-hand advice. A person could only take so much insight. Especially a pregnant person. She didn't want him to stop the therapy. That, she was (as Dr. Fellman would say) "clear on". She just wanted to be...unobserved for a while. Since therapy, Todd was always watching her, pointing things out under the guise of helping her "come into her own as a woman" as he put it. She informed him that she was soon to give birth. How much more into her own as a woman could she come?

It was difficult to admit that sometimes his newfound positivity was positively annoying. She liked what talking to Dr. Fellman had done for Todd, but couldn't his enthusiasm be just a tad less overwhelming? Did he have to do a complete about-face? Was all of his anger going to go away, and was that good? She was comfortable with the Todd she used to know, and afraid that there might be a Todd that she didn't know.

Todd put his hands on Missy's shoulders and spoke quietly. "Now that you mention it, I see your point. Thanks for being so honest—I really appreciate it. Dr. Fellman says that honesty..." He stopped himself. "I'm sorry, there I go again. I promise I won't do it any more. I know why I'm always talking about her, believe it or not. Dr. Fellman warned me. She said it's called transference. There I go again!"

He looked as if a new understanding had just entered his psyche. He was embarrassed, shaking his head and gazing at the kitchen floor. "I'm really sorry. Now that you've pointed this out, I realize how irritating I must be."

Todd hugged her, and Missy forgot to hug him back. She just stood there, stiff in his arms, trying to rethink what had happened. It had all happened so fast. One minute, something was bothering her, and before she knew it she had blurted it out. There was no squirming, no third party to hide behind, just her needs being voiced and a loving husband to hear them. Now Missy hugged Todd back, and both felt a relief. They were becoming the kind of couple that could tell each other anything.

forty one

On Monday night, Diane sat at the desk in her bedroom. In front of her were a blank piece of paper and her old wind-up alarm clock, the latter being the inanimate object that she had chosen to write about for her workshop. She was nervous, but game.

Diane was thinking back to what her teacher had said about the secret to writing. "Listen," he said. *What am I supposed to hear?* She decided to do what her teacher, Larry, had suggested: look at the object and empty her mind. "Let the process happen. That's all you have to do, close your eyes and stand next to your soul." *I paid money for this?* Diane shifted in her seat. Again, she pictured her teacher. She could feel fantasies about him well up and seep out of her before she could yank them back. This was the second time this had happened. Why was she doing this? She did not want to fantasize about this man. He was not her type. He was so…single. *Stop daydreaming and start writing.* Diane picked up her pen, held the point right on the page, and waited. "Don't be in a hurry," she remembered him warning.

Diane closed her eyes and heard ticking. As the moments passed, the ticking seemed more…intrusive. She noticed just the faintest hint of a pang in her stomach. Diane's first impulse was to ignore it. The minute she tried, she heard humming in her head. It was Larry's off-key humming, and with it came his words: "If you feel something, write it down. Even if it's uncomfortable—especially if it's uncomfortable—write it down. As a reader, I don't want to feel safe. In fact, most of the time your reader actually wants to feel things he doesn't normally feel. How else do you account for the success of thrillers, mysteries, and of course the top sellers, True Crime books? Hard to believe, but most people actually do want to get inside the mind of a serial killer, even if it's just during their lunch hour."

Diane stopped thinking about class and went back to the clock, and sure enough, there was another pang in her stomach. This time she was willing to listen. Scared, but willing. She let her pen take her anywhere it wanted to. Before she quite knew what was happening, images attached to feelings seemed to flow from pen to paper.

> As I look at the alarm clock I remember this same clock in a different room in a different time.. I'm sixteen and my parents are gone for a long weekend.
>
> I'm aware that this is my first sexual experience. It must be, because there is a kind of pain between my legs, but I remember him saying that it's all right. It makes me uncomfortable to look at him so I concentrate on the ticking of my alarm clock. I'm embarrassed about what took place. I remember thinking, "I could never do this for a living."
>
> My boyfriend is snoring by now, and even though part of me is glad, part of me thought that

"it" would have more feeling—that I would have more feeling. The ticking of the clock drifts in and out of my consciousness as I mentally dress him with my eyes. As I write these words, I remember how rough his face was when we kissed, I can even still smell the pungent mixture of his body odor and Old Spice cologne. As the theme music to the cologne's commercial plays over and over in my head, I close my eyes. A second later I am startled by the most awful sound in the world—the alarm clock has gone off. But I remember thinking, "I didn't set it. Why is it going off now?"

All of a sudden my boyfriend jumps out of bed and reaches for his clothes, which are scattered all over the floor. I ask him what's going on. "Gotta go toots," is all he says. I realize that he set the alarm. I lay back and watch as he nervously picks up his pants and I see something gold fly out of his pocket and land on the bed next to me. My first thought is how pretty it is and then I am *struck by the object's familiar shape: a round gold band. A wedding band.*

Diane put the pen down. It practically slid out of her hand, for her palms were wet, as were her underarms and forehead.

Like in her memory, the ticking of the clock faded in and out of her consciousness. She remembered now that it took place on a Sunday night and how empty she felt then, and she remembered how much she cried after he left.

Diane looked at the piece of paper in front of her and felt both relief and betrayal. She realized that she had held that memory in for all these years.

●

The next night, Diane sat nervously, waiting for the workshop to begin. She was tired, unable to sleep for most of the night before, uncomfortable with what she had revealed on paper. She still didn't know if she could hand in her assignment. She wrestled with the decision, hesitant to share something so intimate with anyone, least of all someone who already unnerved her. It wasn't her style, raw guts and honesty, at least not with men, but if it would get her an A.... The thought of Larry reading this piece and then knowing something totally and completely honest about her was troublesome. All of her psychology textbooks told her she was wrong, that being open and honest was a sign of strength, not weakness, but somehow it always seemed to be the kind of thing that looked better on paper.

Diane looked up and saw that Larry was motioning for her to come to his desk. She stood up, anxious. Slowly, she walked up to the front of the room.

"Did you want to see me?" asked Diane, assignment in hand.

"Yes, Miss Turner," he said, "I believe you must have left this behind." He gave her back the diary and watched as her face showed relief.

"Oh my God," she said. "I thought I must have left it here, but I came back and it wasn't anywhere, so I just assumed..."

"Miss Turner, I read your diary! I can't tell you how sorry I am. I could not help myself. Please know how sorry I am from the bottom of my heart."

Diane regarded this middle-aged, bald man in front of her, his chubby fingers unadorned. She snapped to attention as he was stuttering something else.

"Of course I've written my Congressman and asked that the laws of privacy be extended to cover personal diaries as well."

Diane stopped him. "Please don't do this to yourself. I didn't write that diary."

"Whose is it?"

"It's the diary of an old woman who died recently," she said.

"Did you know the woman?"

"It's a long story. Just suffice it to say that this woman's diaries were a gift from a...friend, that's all."

"Diaries? You mean there's more?"

"Many more."

"Could I...No, I'm sorry, forget it."

"What? Would you like to read the rest of the diaries? It wouldn't bother me at all. The only thing is, I have to have them back. They've become very important to me."

"I would love to read them. The one that I read was such an experience for me, for a lot of reasons. My grandfather emigrated here from Kebashnik," he said.

"You're kidding!" said Diane. Just then the bell rang and the two were forced to separate.

On her way back to her seat, Diane noticed that she still had her homework assignment in her hand. She looked down at the personal, honest words she held, and considered Larry, sensitive enough to be touched by the diaries. The same ones that touched her. She turned right around and matter-of-factly plunked it down on his desk as he addressed the class.

forty two

A couple of weeks later Larry summoned the courage to call Diane and ask if he might stop by her apartment sometime Saturday afternoon. She nonchalantly agreed, and from noon on kept her eyes glued to her front door, knowing that any minute Larry was going to be knocking. Diane hadn't been this nervous in years. *What is it about him that rattles me so?* She was certain that she was not really attracted to him—so why the sexy underwear?

Diane heard the rap at the door and jumped up.

"Hi Larry," she said, unable to look him in the eye as she opened her door. "Would you like to come in?" She wasn't used to this. It was strange to be ushering a single man into her apartment who wasn't there to deliver a pizza or something. The awkwardness she felt was making her mouth dry. She just couldn't relax.

"Hi Diane—may I call you Diane?" he asked.

"Sure," she managed through her nerves. "Please, sit down," she said, eyes fixed on the floor.

Larry was confused, and for a second he thought she wanted him to take a seat on the blue carpet. He looked up and saw her motioning toward the couch. Relieved, he moved toward it. "There is so much—oh, before I forget, Diane—here you are," he said, handing her something.

"My homework assignment." She had forgotten all about it. The intimate content of the pages came back to her all at once and she suddenly felt warm all over. Larry eagerly pointed out the A at the top of the page.

"Diane, I have to tell you, this was wonderful work—truly. I hope you know why it was so good."

"Because you said it was?" she asked, staring at the A.

He smiled. "Diane has no idea how charming she is, which makes her even more attractive," he thought resignedly, aware of the sad fact that she would never run naked on the shores of Tahiti with him. He stepped back into his scholarly suit. "Knowing why a piece of writing is good is just as important as having talent. And you, Diane, have talent," he said.

Upon hearing the word talent, Diane lost all sense of embarrassment.

"You think I have talent?" she asked. In all her years, no one had ever said that to her. Even with her recent recovered memories she couldn't recall anyone ever saying such a thing to her. Or maybe they had. Maybe she just hadn't heard it.

"Yes. I think you have lots of it. You did just what I asked you to do—you surrendered yourself to the moment, just like someone does when they laugh, and it was wonderful. If you're this good now, over time you'll be remarkable. I mean that with all my heart."

Again, she felt that same sense of being attracted to him, like she did the other night at class. Only right now it was much more potent. "I can't do this, fantasize about someone like him. This is insane… Maybe we could have an affair," she thought. "An affair…but wait, is it still considered an affair if both people are single? I wonder how that works?"

"Are those the rest of the diaries?" Larry asked, noticing the box next to the coffee table that held them, and thankful for something he could talk to her about. For the rest of the afternoon and into the small of the evening, if at all possible.

"Yes," she said, walking over to the box.

"Tell me something, Diane. How did you come upon these wonderful diaries? I'll bet that in itself is an interesting story," he smiled, waiting.

"You said that your own grandfather emigrated here from Kebashnik," she said.

"Yes," he stumbled. "As I was reading I couldn't believe it. It was like my grandfather was alive again and telling me the same stories about Kebashnik that used to put me to sleep." Larry caught himself. "I didn't mean that the way it sounded. See, every night he would tuck me in and I would beg him to tell me all about Kebashnik."

"He sounds like a wonderful man," said Diane. "Was his last name the same as yours, York?"

"No," said Larry. "When he got to Ellis Island it was changed to York."

"What was it originally?"

"It was Yorvik. Slak Yorvik."

forty three

Across the courtyard of his apartment complex, Larry's neighbors noticed that he was humming more than ever now. They were pleased to note that the overall content of his music was different. Showtunes were out—love songs were in.

He looked forward to reading another diary and was just settling in on the couch to do so. Larry opened it to the first page and began.

Dear Diary,
Today my secret love Slak Yorvik

Larry stared at the page in utter disbelief. "This cannot be my grandfather. Maybe Slak Yorvik is a common Kebashnik name like John Smith is here. No wonder Diane had that funny look on her face when I said my grandfather's name."

He quickly turned back to the page, eager to absorb its contents.

Today my secret love Slak Yorvik left for the island of America with his wife and cow. They let him take the cow on the ship because he is royalty. Oh diary, I wish so much that I was royalty, so that I could be married to Slak instead of that pig he married. Now he is traveling to America with a pig and a cow. I have made a vow that I will somehow get the money to follow **S**lak to America. I don't know how I will get it or where it will come from, but I will do it. I will never stop loving my **S**lak. Somehow, I know that this is the right thing to do. I am hoping to be his mistress once I catch up with him.

To be honest, I'm not exactly sure that **S**lak knows who I am. **W**e only smiled at each other the one time on the way to the fish factory, but I know it is our destiny to be together forever, or at least be able to meet once a week in secret. For now I'll be content to just hope that his wife catches something bad from the cow and it makes her too tired to have physical relations with him.

"This must be the earliest case of stalking ever recorded," thought Larry, quickly turning the page.

forty four

Estelle looked younger. The weight that she had gained smoothed out a lot of wrinkles in her face, which thrilled her. She was also just a little bit infatuated with Allan. They had been spending a lot of time together in recent weeks.

While they were having lunch one day, Allan talked Estelle into taking a natural childbirth class. It took a lot of convincing though; she told him how much she was counting on getting gas. Allan gently informed his older lunchmate that hospitals no longer gave women gas during labor. When Allan promised to be her coach, she gave in. He told her that he believed in her, that he knew she could do it. Estelle was not used to believing in herself. The concept was foreign to her. "In my day, we didn't think about self-esteem. We went to church instead."

Estelle was quite flattered by Allan's interest in her. How he listened to her, encouraging her to talk about things that troubled her. Today, while they were out to lunch, she did.

"I know people don't like me and I don't care," she said, half-thinking, over her Coquille St. Jacques.

"Estelle, that's not true. Come on, let's be honest," he stopped, swallowed hard, and continued. "Look, I hope you don't take this the wrong way. Freud said that a negation is as good as a confirmation."

Estelle put her fork down and patted her lipstick with her white cloth napkin. Something got lost in the translation. She didn't mean for him to take her small comment seriously. He was supposed to smile, nod and move on to an interesting topic. This was no good. She was just throwing him a bone, but no more than that. Suddenly, she felt irritated.

Allan felt the birth of a single bead of perspiration on his forehead as he cautiously continued. "What I mean is that I've come to believe that whenever someone says something like, 'oh...it's not that I don't like her, it's just that...' what they really mean is that they don't like her." Softly, he continued. "And when you say 'I know people don't like me but I don't care...'" He paused, wincing. "I think you do care." He finally breathed and managed to wipe the perspiration from his brow.

Estelle was silent, and now wished desperately that she hadn't said a word, but she realized that she wanted to please him, and yet she could not, *would* not do this.

"I changed my mind—I don't want to talk about this. Check, please."

Allan saw Estelle's spotted hands tremble and instantly regretted saying anything, but something nagged at him to continue. He decided to, for Estelle's sake.

"It's okay to admit you're hurt."

"I'm too old for this," she thought, and for the first time since he had gone, she longed for her husband, envying him sitting beside a pool with retired people, people their own age, people who could make a Highball from memory.

"Estelle, please, with all due respect, you're my friend. You matter to me. But I can't lie. I think that you do care if people don't like you. It's okay. Look, I'll admit it to you: I care what people think. There, I said it."

Suddenly, Estelle looked around impatiently for the snotty waitress who was nowhere in sight, but would doubtless be expecting a big tip.

"Why won't you talk to me?" asked Allan.

"All you young people do is talk about your feelings," she sniped. But then she stopped. Estelle wanted to let him have it, but found that she couldn't. This was Allan, this was her White Knight, this was the person whose voice on the radio had made her feel young again. He'd been with her in her thoughts since before she was pregnant—hell, he was the reason she was pregnant! After all, she had gone into the hospital to find him.

Allan reached across the table and took Estelle's trembling hand. "It's okay. We can talk about something else."

Instead of relief, Estelle felt surprisingly disappointed at his changing the subject. She felt empty, as if she had let him down. Looking at him now, she realized that she could not keep up with him or his generation—they both demanded too much. Once again, she retreated to the image of Todd Senior, retired, and found solace. She ached in a small way for him, which shocked her. She ached for the simplicity of what they used to be. Todd Senior never demanded intimacy from her, that's why their marriage had lasted so long. Or had it?

In a sudden moment of understanding, she realized just then that Todd Senior had felt free to leave, perhaps compelled to leave because of her resistance to owning up to any intimate feelings.

Estelle estimated her White Knight. Now she really had to give him something, something more than just a bone. She decided that she could do it. Somehow, she would extract some molecule of feeling that she would rather keep hidden from the rest of the world and expose it to him. That would make him happy.

"Allan," said Estelle.

He looked up from his all-egg-white omelet.

"Yes?"

"My first baby was stillborn."

forty five

Missy and Todd were in the family room watching television. All of a sudden Missy turned to Todd and said, "I don't feel so good."

"Do you want to go upstairs?" he asked, taking her hand.

"I don't mean that. I think there's something wrong with the baby," she said.

Todd felt panic sweep through his whole body. Without saying a word he rushed to the phone and called Dr. Bern, Missy's obstetrician.

Todd watched as Missy sat with the phone up to her ear, listening to her doctor. Millions and millions of images went through his mind, some were good, some were bad. Some were based in reality, others were total delusions founded in paranoia, still others were a healthy jaunt into escapism to ease his troubled mind. The instant his wife hung up the phone Todd made up his mind that whatever it was, he could handle it. He realized that he wanted to be there for his wife, and now for the first time in his life, he knew that he could.

"Dr. Bern said there's nothing to worry about," said Missy.

"Thank God for His mercy," cried Todd, taking Missy in his arms.

"But she does think that I should see her first thing Monday morning, just to be sure."

●

Missy and Todd sat nervously in her obstetrician's waiting room. Both jumped when the nurse called out Missy's name.

"The doctor will see you now," she informed them, opening the door to the examining room.

Twenty minutes later, Missy, Todd, and their doctor came out of the room laughing. "I had a feeling it was nothing," said Dr. Bern.

"I'm so relieved that I can't even tell you," said Missy.

Todd nodded.

"Good, I'm glad everything checked out. You're at six and a half months right now, and we'll need to keep a close eye on you until you deliver. I want you to come in every week from now until the birth," smiled the doctor.

"Why?" asked Todd. "Do you know something we don't?"

"There's probably a lot I know that you don't," said Dr. Bern. "After all, I am a doctor. I just don't want to take any chances. That's all it is, I promise."

forty six

Estelle often thought about what she had said to Allan that day at lunch.

The words hung heavy in her mind, pulling her down like so many of her weighty beaded dresses. Allan was the first person in her life who didn't seem afraid of her and Estelle didn't know exactly how to deal with it. She realized she'd have to change her strategy with Allan. Instead of intimidation through abuse, she'd have to go another route. She would have to meter out small amounts of her own personal pain to keep him interested. That's why she blurted out what she did about her first baby. She didn't want to—she hadn't, in all the years since it had happened. She couldn't understand why people would ever want to re-live horrible things all over again when they could smoke instead. Well, she had given him an earful that day.

Estelle had ordered him not to tell a soul of what she had confessed. "You take that to your grave," she demanded. She had only done it as strategy. Estelle happily remembered that that was all she would say on the subject. She showed Allan that she had no adolescent need to cry about something she couldn't do anything about anyway. Although she had to admit, only to herself of course, that since she had appeased Allan, she felt a little less…crowded, inside, in the place where she stored her thoughts and troubles.

forty seven

By now the members of Brave Women were very used to seeing a man routinely take his place in the half-W. Estelle always raced to sit next to him. She was very possessive of Allan. He was hers.

It was a few minutes before the meeting was to begin and the room was abuzz with comfortable chit-chat. Judy had a question for Allan, and shifted her sitting position to catch his eye.

Estelle took note.

"What nursing program were you in, Allan?" Judy asked.

Estelle felt a hatred well up underneath her shiny blouse. She shuffled in her seat. "Oh God, are we starting this nonsense again?"

A sudden hush befell the room.

Missy closed her eyes. She didn't feel well, and this certainly wasn't going to help.

"Start what again?" asked Kyle.

"Please Kyle, I can speak for myself," said Judy. "What do you mean by nonsense, Estelle?"

Estelle forged ahead, unable to stop herself, knowing she was making Allan angry. "What I mean, exactly, is that we've heard this song before! This is the same old story of your life and we've already read it!"

Everyone looked at each other, then back at Estelle, who seemed perfectly satisfied that she had clarified herself.

Allan spoke up. "Estelle, I'm not sure we know what you mean. Could you please explain?"

Exasperation emanated from Estelle as she made another attempt to clarify. "Judy claimed she was going to attend medical school and she never did. Now, suddenly, out of the blue, she wants to become a female nurse! Tell me Judy, why the sudden interest in medicine?"

"Sudden interest? I'm already a veterinarian. I'd hardly call that a sudden interest. I just thought if I didn't have the money for more medical school, maybe nursing was the best solution. Not that it's any of your business, but I realize now I'd like to have patients that are able to talk back to me."

Eager to move as far away from this collaborative confrontation as she could, Diane spoke. "Well, why don't we start the meeting now? Does anyone have anything they'd like to share with the group?"

"I think we'd all like to share our mutual loathing for Estelle," said Kyle.

"I'll second that," Missy thought privately.

"Okay, then," said Diane. "I guess I'll start. I got an A on my…"

"Estelle," said Allan, "What are you doing?"

"I'm sure I don't know what you mean," stated Estelle, icily.

"I'm sure you do. Estelle, come on, it's time we were all honest. You have a habit of provoking people. Now what's that about?" asked Allan.

"It's not provocation, it's progesterone," Estelle fumbled.

"Don't blame this on hormones! Remember, I'm a male nurse," said Allan. "Now come on, at least care enough about yourself to be honest. Why did you start a fight with Judy?"

Estelle said nothing.

"All right," he continued, "I want you to know that you and I are friends, special friends, and that will never change. I love you."

The group looked back at Estelle. They saw that she was scared.

Estelle could feel all eyes, looking, waiting. "Damn it to hell!" she thought. She was too tired to fight anymore. The pregnancy was making her exhausted. She didn't have the stamina she used to. Something hard in her began to crumble. The others looked on in amazement as they saw a tiny tear begin to form in the corner of Estelle's left eye.

"Go ahead and cry if you want, it's okay," said Allan. The others were all standing by with emergency hugs.

It had been thirty-five years since Estelle had cried, and right now she wasn't sure that she could, though she wanted to desperately. The others watched as Estelle tried to force the tears out, but she was having trouble—there were too many of them struggling to get out, like someone just yelled fire in a crowded theater.

"Just take your time," said Diane gently. "Just close your eyes and let go."

Estelle tried with all her might to force them out, but they wouldn't budge. Finally, Estelle looked down and saw the age spots on her trembling hands and that's what finally did it. She was just a tired old woman that no one liked. She began to sob—deep, heavy sobs; and to her amazement, it felt wonderful.

They watched as Estelle wept. Diane sensed that these were old tears, a long time in the making. Her cries were too heavy, too labored, for them to be about anything in the present. She reached out and took Estelle's hand. Allan moved closer and placed her head on his chest.

Kyle and Judy noticed a shift in their feelings for Estelle. It was inevitable—their vision of her couldn't help but be affected by this sudden display of vulnerability. Judy realized that everyone struggles, and that no matter how grating a person is, everyone is human. Even Estelle.

Soon all the women and Allan gave Estelle a lengthy group hug, and only quit because her strong perfume began to make some of them dizzy.

The ladies watched as a slightly different Estelle emerged from the group hug. Gone were the affected mannerisms that they all knew and hated. The Estelle in front of them now seemed smaller, physically, not as tight-faced, and, oddly, a little younger.

"I want to say something. I'd like to apologize, Judy," said Estelle, her hands still trembling. "I-I got jealous that you were talking to Allan," she paused, as if trying to sort something out. "I guess I must have reverted to sarcasm to cover my feelings." Estelle turned to Diane. "Is that what I did?"

"According to all my textbooks," she answered.

"And my self-help books," said Judy.

"And last night's television documentary on dysfunctional women in their early sixties," said Kyle.

"Not to get off the subject, but very briefly, could someone take me to the hospital?" asked Missy.

The others turned quickly. Allan reached in his nurse's travel kit for his stethoscope. "Everyone stand back. Diane, get an ambulance here right now!"

"I'd better call Todd," said Estelle. "Junior and Senior."

Just then Missy lost consciousness.

"Maybe it's just the shock of seeing Estelle apologize," said Kyle, hopefully.

"I don't think so," said Allan as he quickly checked her pulse. "I wish it were."

As she watched them take Missy out of the room, Estelle really began to cry.

forty eight

As Todd was saying good-bye to Dr. Fellman after another session in which they both agreed that his fears about Missy and the baby were unwarranted and most likely didn't mean anything, Dr. Fellman's secretary came rushing in.

"Todd, I'm sorry to interrupt, but your mother's calling…"

"Oh my God, something is wrong!" He went to the phone and simply said, "I'm on my way." And he was.

Missy's obstetrician walked into the visitor's lounge and encountered the expectant faces of Estelle, Todd, Diane, Kyle, Judy and Allan.

"The news isn't good," said Dr. Bern, looking directly into the eyes of each and every person. "The problem is…" Just then Dr. Bern noticed Allan standing among Missy's family and friends. "Hi Allan," she said awkwardly, inwardly cursing herself for not wearing lip-liner today of all days. Dr. Bern continued. "I'm sorry. The problem is that at almost seven months it's too soon to take the baby, but if we wait, we chance losing it. All we can do is wait and hope for the best. The good news is that Missy is very strong, physically, and I can almost guarantee you, Todd, that you will have children—even if this one doesn't make it. But for now it's touch-and-go, so why don't we just wait and see?"

No one knew anything more that night. Everyone except Todd went home. He insisted on sleeping on a cot next to Missy.

Allan also stayed, asking to be put on duty so he could care for Missy personally and make sure that no mistakes happened.

Kyle and Judy held each other the whole night, glad for each other's comfort.

Estelle cried herself to sleep that night, having done so only once before, the night the doctors told her and Todd Senior that their baby had died.

Diane went back to her apartment upset, scared, and lonely. She wanted someone to talk to, but could not think of who she could really open up to. Yet somewhere in the back of her mind, slowly, a name surfaced. Larry, her teacher. At first, she dismissed it as low blood sugar (she was dieting). But then, even after she had eaten, his name kept popping into her mind. She decided to listen to whatever was saying his name. She looked his number up and dialed it. She was nervous. Or was it excitement? "Why am I calling him? He's obviously not interested. He never called me after that Saturday that he stopped over." Diane stopped and realized that the minute he seemed uninterested...

"Hello?" answered Larry, half asleep.

"Hi," said Diane.

"You're gonna have to give me more than that to go on if I'm going to recognize your voice," said Larry.

"Sorry, I guess I was embarrassed. I obviously woke you up. It's Diane."

His voice brightened considerably. "Hi. What's new?"

Diane felt better just hearing his voice. "I..." Somehow she didn't want to go into everything that happened. "I was just wondering—how are you?" She winced at her own words.

"I assume this is what it's like to have a concussion—I know you're supposed to wake the person periodically and ask how they are," he said, attempting to impress her with some groggy humor. "Sorry, Diane, that was stupid. It's amazing how wit is the first thing to go when you're tired. I'm beginning to wake up now."

"Look, I don't want to bother you. I'm really sorry."

"You've already bothered me," he said, trying to comfort her. "Diane, I can hear in your voice that you need to talk. Now something's the matter—please, tell me what it is."

They conversed all night, Diane never even mentioning anything about Missy. Larry told her about how he thought his grandfather was Slak Yorvik, the same man as the one in Yelena's diaries.

"How do you know it's the same guy? There must be a million Kebashnik men named Slak Yorvik," said Diane.

"I know because in her diaries Yelena talks about Slak's wife having died on the ship on the way to America—something about being kicked by a cow—and how bad she felt. My grandfather's first wife died on their way to this country."

"I can't believe it…that's so weird!" she said.

"She also describes Slak's head—how it was larger than most—and my grandfather was very sensitive about the size of his head. That's why he always wore hats—even in summer. Now that can't be a coincidence," Larry insisted.

Diane agreed, and they made a date to go through more of the diaries together—at Larry's place. He was adamant that he wanted to make dinner for her. At first Diane hesitated, she hadn't had a date outside of her apartment in years. The concept of dating someone she could be seen in public with was strange to her. She slowly agreed and the two finally hung up as dawn was breaking.

forty nine

Dr. Bern, Missy's obstetrician, told her she'd have to stay in the hospital until labor could safely be induced. At seven months, the earliest they could take the baby was still five weeks away. Todd, of course, was worried sick, and to top it all off he'd have to live alone with Estelle. Todd once warned Missy never to leave him alone with his mother—he didn't say why. Of course that was before therapy, and before Estelle learned to cry at the Brave Women meeting, and before Allan became her friend. Sweet Allan, he insisted on being Missy's nurse, and, even though he was trained as a surgical nurse and had no experience working with maternity patients, the hospital didn't seem to mind. In fact, it seemed to Missy that most of the hospital staff seemed afraid of Allan, as if…as if he had something on them?

As Dr. Bern was leaving Missy's room, Allan was walking down the hall writing something in a notebook about a possible baby mix-up, when the two bumped into each other.

"I'm sorry, I—Allan! Well, hello," said Dr. Bern, removing her stethoscope because it was covering up her pearls.

"Hi Callie," he said. Allan inched back. He hadn't been alone with her in a long time. He had managed to keep his distance even though he was one of Missy's nurses. Now Allan didn't quite know what to say.

She removed her glasses.

"God, she's pretty," he thought.

Callie took a half step toward him and quietly slipped on the silver earrings that she kept in the pocket of her lab coat.

"She just keeps getting prettier," he thought. Allan always believed that Callie was the type of woman who would get more attractive with age, not less. For a brief second he wondered why they ever broke up.

"Still threatening to write that tell-all book?" she asked.

Now he remembered why they broke up. When Allan had informed Callie about all the hospital errors that he had chronicled, she didn't want to hear about it. She didn't want to know about a doctor taking a donor heart from someone who never donated it. Callie didn't want to listen, didn't want to acknowledge that this type of thing was happening at St. Martina's, much less testify against a fellow doctor in court. Allan was dumbfounded, especially because the victim was a second cousin of Callie's.

"Still doing Nautilus?" she asked, taking her hair out of its barrette.

He used to be so in awe of her when they were dating. Not because she was a doctor and he just a male nurse. Allan had fallen deeply in love with her. Once again, when they were seeing each other, he had put the woman he loved on a pedestal. He realized now, after a number of Brave Women meetings, that to him, in regards to women, everything was an either/or situation. They were either perfect in every way, or they were only imperfect. It was that simple, that black-and-white for Allan, and always had been. He realized now that he never allowed anyone he dated any flaws.

Thinking back, it occurred to him that Callie must have been afraid to testify against a fellow doctor in court, especially a superior. But, as usual, at the first sign of fear in a female he had panicked. It all went back to his image of women.

Now he saw Callie standing in front of him, and for the first time in his life, the idea of accepting a woman he was attracted to, faults and all, didn't frighten him.

"Now that we're alone, I want to say that Missy is my

friend—she's very dear to me. And if anything happens to her, I will go after this hospital with everything I've got. That's a promise."

He turned and walked away as Dr. Bern was struggling to remove her white lab coat, holding Missy's chart between her teeth.

●

Estelle phoned her husband. It was the first time they had spoken in a year. He had regained his former Texas accent, which surprised and somewhat delighted Estelle.

"What's new, darlin'?" he asked, glad to hear from her.

She thought about his question. "A lot," she began, informing him about Missy and her situation, Todd's therapy, and her own pregnancy. "What's new with you?" she asked.

Slowly, they began to talk again.

fifty

Diane stood in her bathroom surrounded by all of her moisturizers, and in one quick movement of her arm swept them into her garbage. She wasn't really sure why she had done that. *They're taking up too much space* was what occurred to her, but somehow that didn't seem to be the reason.

The other day in a department store, when Diane accidentally caught a reflection of herself in the mirror under fluorescent lights, she didn't scream inside. Usually, fluorescent lights were responsible for intense panic followed by an irrational need to purchase more moisturizer. But that didn't happen this time. She thought about it for a minute, but then her mind drifted dreamily back to Larry, and Diane found herself wandering out of the store.

It was strange having Brave Women meetings without Missy. The first two weeks they all spent the entire time saying nice things about Missy—even Estelle, who also confessed to having called her husband in Texas. Allan was always there giving progress reports on Missy's condition, so they got their information first hand and didn't worry as much.

Kyle and Judy were going to try artificial insemination again. Estelle suggested they just both go in and have some moles removed and "see what happens."

Estelle's own pregnancy was going just fine, surprisingly. Diane found herself looking at Estelle's abdomen covetously. Judy suggested that they make one of their meetings a shower for Estelle and everyone thought it was a good idea.

fifty one

Diane was nervous as she stood outside Larry's apartment (he had invited her over to dinner) holding a large box filled with diaries. She could hear his humming through the door, which she remembered used to bother her a great deal, and which now, oddly enough, only slightly irritated her.

"Hi," sang Larry as he opened the door. "I'm just setting the table. Here, let me take those for you." He set the box down and went back to the dining room.

Diane walked in and looked around, closing the door. "He's messy," she thought. Then she realized she had no point of reference. She had never been to a date's home, because her dates were always married. "Maybe he's neat by comparison—how do I know?" she wondered, continuing to look around.

It was a charming old apartment with iron radiators and wood everywhere. Upon further inspection, Diane realized that it wasn't messy, it was homey. She surveyed the living room. The hardwood floors were a beautiful dark brown, with country throw-rugs here and there. Hanging on the wall behind the television set was a patchwork quilt. This was not what Diane had expected. What had she expected? She didn't know. In fact, she was only aware of certain things that she hadn't anticipated. His apartment was so...decorated, so deliberate in its flavor, its charm. This was surprising, and very appealing. Diane couldn't help but be even more curious about Larry. She didn't know that men liked quilts. She wondered where he got it. Did he collect them? An odd hobby for a man if he did. Perhaps it was a gift from an old girlfriend. "That would be better," she thought. Diane stopped. Her criteria for the kind of man she could keep company with was so stringent, she was realizing. So what if he collected quilts? Why would that throw me? Just then she noted something that had been tugging at her since the minute she walked in the door. The way she felt. That was the second thing she hadn't anticipated: how she would feel when she walked in the door of this enigmatic man's apartment—like she belonged.

Larry was still in the dining room setting the table. "I fixed a native Kebashnik dish that my grandfather used to make every Sunday. It's a sausage, egg and cream cheese casserole. I hope you like it," Larry shouted.

She walked into the dining room but didn't hear him. Diane was looking at the center of the dining room table, where Larry had placed the most beautiful bouquet of fresh-cut lilacs. He saw her notice them. "I knew you liked lilacs because I saw them at your place." He walked over to her and said, "Diane, forgive me if I stare, but you have the most beautiful skin."

They made love before dinner and after dinner, and in between Larry read to her from the diaries by the light of the fire. A real fire.

fifty two

Missy's baby died. It was no one's fault, Allan assured everyone. "I know because, thank God, I was there. If it makes anyone feel any better, for the first time in twenty years the hospital was not to blame. I made sure that they did everything they could."

Tonight, everyone was at the Brave Women meeting except, of course, Missy. Estelle, grateful that she had learned to cry, was crying. She herself was due in three months, and she told the group how guilty she felt about having her own baby. That was what she told the group, and it was true, but she had stopped short of telling them the whole truth. Estelle's current guilt was mixed up with her memory of the guilt she felt when her first baby was born dead thirty-five years ago. The doctors told her it wasn't because of anything she did until they were blue in the face. It didn't matter. It happened, that was the sad fact that nobody could take away. She wasn't ever going to take her little girl home. And no one would ever know how she felt, so what was the point, anyway, of talking about the sadness she harbored? Estelle remembered dismissing the event and everything that went with it.

Now, when she thought of Missy...actually, thought wasn't the right word. Estelle could feel what Missy was feeling. She was the only one, she realized. Estelle recalled when she used to fantasize about the relationship she would have with her future daughter-in-law, whomever she might be. How she imagined that Todd's new wife would see her as a font of wisdom that she could tap into. Estelle thought about that daydream, so innocent at the time. Now the fantasy shifted into a sad reality.

fifty three

Diane and Larry had been dating regularly for the last eight weeks. When she stopped to consider what was happening—that she was actually seeing someone who was single—Diane felt the panic start. It was so foreign to her, the openness, the honesty.

There were no boundaries in this relationship—it was at once splendid and terrifying. Larry made it obvious how much he cared for her. He seemed completely uninhibited in his feelings for her. There was a straightforward quality about this man that she wasn't used to, and it alarmed her. Paradoxically, though, she had to admit that it was a relief to be able to trust someone so completely.

Sometimes Diane wondered how the whole thing came about, because it seemed to have happened so out of the blue. Previous efforts to force herself to be attracted to an available man, a suitable male, had always backfired. She couldn't help but wonder why. Why this time?

She had found herself wanting to talk to someone, someone other than the members of Brave Women, whose emotions concerning Missy and her loss were too fresh and unstable. As an outsider, Larry was able to listen to Diane without his own emotional needs getting in the way. She was touched by his capacity to empathize, and his philosophical view of life and death gave her some perspective on the situation that even helped in the meetings. He wasn't bad in bed, either.

It was after the workshop. Larry was walking Diane to her car, and just as he was leaning over to kiss her, they both heard a man's voice.

"Diane?"

It was Joe Della Femina.

"Hi," was all he said.

As Diane stood there, gazing into this man's eyes, it wasn't hard for Larry to sense that his days were numbered.

"I left my wife," said Joe.

"Joe Della Femina, I'd like you to meet Larry York," she said politely. "So…"

"So," said Larry, "anybody hungry?"

"I did it for you. I left her for you, Diane," he continued as if it was just the two of them.

"I don't know what to say..."

"Don't say anything now, just tell me you'll think about us again," he said.

"I can't," Diane said. "I'm through with guys like you. If you cheated on your wife you'll eventually cheat on me."

"That's true. I can't tell you how many times I've read that," said Larry.

"Don't you believe I'm different?" asked Joe.

"No," said Larry.

"Larry, could you excuse us, please?" asked Diane.

"Sure. I'll see you later, I hope."

Diane watched him walk away and turned back to Joe.

"What do you want?"

"I want us back."

"Your wife finally kicked you out, didn't she?"

"Yes, but that has nothing to do with this. I was going to leave her anyway. I just let her think it was her idea. See how sensitive I turned out to be? Come on, don't over-analyze everything—for once in your life do something spontaneous."

"I'm going to have to say good-night now."

"Come on. What? It's not that Larry, is it? That's easy, I'll just tell his wife…"

"He's not married."

"You're dating someone who's not married?"

Diane nodded.

"Well then, you can date me—I'm not married anymore either."

"You're not understanding something," she said. "I don't want to date you."

He laughed. "Yes you do. You know why? Because guys like me are in your blood, Diane. We both know you could never go for a dork like that Larry."

Diane was beginning to feel uncomfortable. Part of her started to react as if he was touching her without being invited.

"Please leave."

"Okay. But we both know the real you, Diane." He turned and walked away.

For a couple of weeks Diane avoided answering her phone, not just because Joe might call, but, she realized, she was also afraid to talk to Larry. She was terrified that Joe was right about her. "Could I really be turned off by nice guys?"

Joe sent her presents: lacy bras, sexy panties, flimsy negligées. Larry sent her poetry and original love sonnets. For the first time in her life, Diane prayed for an answer. It came in two parts. The first was when Diane was randomly leafing through one of the diaries. Yelena talked about something pertinent:

> Dear Diary,
> Now that I am in America, Slak
> has finally come around. He mourned
> his wife's and cow's deaths for a

year. He has begun to court me,
bringing me American candies and wool
blankets. But now, the strangest thing
has happened: the more Slak courts me,
the less I like him. It is so odd,
because I know that I used to love
him.

And another thing has happened. I
met another man. He too is from
Kebashnik, and is very wealthy. He
owns the sausage plant where I now
work. I have heard from other workers that he is mean, but I do not
believe it. He told me that he would
like to take me to the Kebashnik Ballet
which is appearing here for one night
only. I told him yes. Somehow I feel
like I should not do this, but find I
cannot help myself. Which one shall I
choose?

All the old tapes in Diane's head demanded that she go
back to Joe. He was what she knew, all she knew, and there
was comfort in the familiar. It was tempting to regress. It
was a kind of emotional recidivism, and she knew it, but
still, the familiar was very potent. Diane thought about
Larry, and about how strange it felt to have dates in public.
There was no drama, no thrill of knowing that her date was
risking his marriage just to be with her. It was all so open
and above-board, so ordinary.

Except for how she felt. That was, she had to admit,
extraordinary. But, as Diane was finding out, with new feel-

ings, no matter how wonderful, came…effort. The effort of adjusting. Who was she now? So much energy had, in the past, been expended on keeping her insecurities at bay. Now everything in her consciousness was shifting and she would have to adapt. Larry made her feel so…complete. For the first time in her life she felt a general happiness. She definitely wasn't used to seeing herself that way.

fifty four

"My mother is different now," announced Todd at a therapy session.

"Different?" asked Dr. Fellman.

"She's not as critical, I've noticed."

"Maybe you're the one who's different," said the doctor.

Todd thought for a moment. "Maybe, but so is she. My mother seems a little more...fragile. Yes, definitely. Missy noticed it too. In fact, she cries at the drop of a hat now. Missy says it's just all the hormones, but I don't think so. I think it's something else."

"Like what?"

"I think it's all the meetings."

"Meetings?"

"I told you that she and Missy go to these women's meetings and you're supposed to cry a lot. I don't know if it's all the crying or hormones or what, but I don't dread being around her as much. It's a nice change."

"Did you think about what I said before, Todd? About ending therapy?" asked Dr. Fellman.

"I've thought about it, and I think it's not one of your better ideas."

She smiled. "You know that you don't really need me anymore, don't you?"

"I guess," he said reluctantly.

"Do you think that you'll try to have another baby?"

"I want to, but I don't think Missy would ever try again. I told her whatever she decides..."

fifty five

Diane opened her door and found Larry standing in her hallway.

"Could I talk to you?" he asked.

"Come on in," she said.

"You haven't been to the workshop the last few weeks," he said. "Quite frankly, I don't think you're at the level that you can be playing hooky, if you know what I mean. Yes, you have improved," he acknowledged, nodding his head, "but not that much."

Diane smiled.

"And it's just that I was thinking this whole awkward triangle thing would make a great story. I'm sure it sounds strange to you, but writers often have tragic lives. It's not a requirement, but it helps, believe me," he said.

"Well, Larry, thanks for the advice. Maybe someday I'll write about it."

"Actually, I was talking about myself. In fact, I've already written of my pain and sent it off to *GQ*. They told me they liked it, but it was no story until it had an ending. So I came to see if there was an ending yet...Diane?"

"I don't know what to say. I've never been in this position before in my life," she said.

"I have, many times," he noted. "Of course, it's always been from this angle."

She laughed, and it made him glad.

"I just thought you wanted what I wanted," he said.

"How could I want what you want? I don't even know what it is that I want. Do you want something to drink?"

He walked toward Diane and quietly kissed her.

An hour later as they were lying in bed, Larry suddenly

sat up.

"I want to marry you."

No one had ever said anything like that to Diane before in her life. The closest thing had been "I'm married, you?" She took a deep breath, and before she could exhale Larry kissed her again.

"Well? Do I have an ending for my magazine article? They pretty much promised me that if we ended up married they'd publish it."

"I don't..."

"Please Diane, I've never been published before."

Diane turned to him and started to cry. She immediately stopped herself because of her complexion. Fortunately, not one single drop ever slid down her face—Larry was there with his hanky, catching them all, gently whispering. "You're much too lovely to have a face full of tears." Of course that made her cry even more. In fact, the more he vowed that she would never shed another tear as long as he was around, the more she cried, and he caught every teardrop.

"I'm afraid my hanky is soaked," said Larry.

"I'm sorry," she cried.

"Don't be sorry. For God's sake, that's what it's there for. I'm just glad that I have a clean one for once."

"No," Diane corrected, "I don't know if I can marry you."

"Oh," he said, beginning to cry himself.

The two lovers lay in bed, crying side by side, sharing a sopping hanky.

"Look, don't feel pressure to marry me just because of the story. I'll make up some other ending. I'll say that you died suddenly."

"Part of me wants to marry you. But you're just so much

the opposite kind of guy that I could ever picture myself with."

"You really must come back to class, if only for the sentence structure," he said, kissing her. "I promise I won't bother you. I just want what's best for you."

"You're so thoughtful," Diane sighed.

"Guys like me have to be thoughtful. We literally have no choice. Believe me, if I had hair…"

"If you had hair you would still be thoughtful and I know it," Diane said.

"Yes, but I could change."

She laughed.

"I love to see you laugh," he said, stroking her hair. "I want to marry you. I want to have your child—is that too much? Am I being too nice again?"

"What am I going to do?"

"Well," said Larry, "Hopefully you've got enough depth as a person to not make a decision based on chest hair. Hopefully, the words "serial infidelity" mean at least something to you. If not, I'm sunk."

After Larry left, Diane opened the diary sitting on the dresser next to her bed.

Dear Diary,
It was last night that I snuck out with Mr. Sheshonyik. (He owns the American sausage plant where I now work.) All night I prayed that Slak would not see us. It was risky, because I told Slak I was sick from the heavy American diet and could not accompany him on the egg walk like we

had planned.

Oh diary, what a night I had! Mr.
Sheshonyik is so rich! And so
American! He has never even milked a
cow in his life! You can tell that just
by looking at his hands. He doesn't
have to, because he has so much money.
Oh, how I want to be just like him. I
want to be American.

I hope with all my heart that Mr.
Sheshonyik likes me too–although when I
really think about it, why would he? If
I can get him to marry me I would be
so lucky. Maybe then he would stop
calling me worker number 6794 in
front of other people.

"How can she put up with that kind of abuse?" thought
Diane. But she knew, because she had been putting up with
abuse of a different sort for years.

Why did she want to go back to Joe? she asked herself.
Besides the fact that it was what she knew, there was something else. Maybe Larry liked her more than she liked herself, which brought into focus the fact that she didn't like
herself very much. At least Joe's opinion matched up.

fifty six

Estelle was a month from her due date. Dr. Gore advised her to exercise to bring down her blood pressure, which was a little high. "Something low impact," she said. "Walking or swimming."

Estelle chose swimming and joined the local Y. The closer to delivery she got, the more anxiety-ridden she became. "My god," she thought, "What if I'm swimming and my water breaks? How will I know?" Such were the questions with which Estelle awoke her obstetrician in the middle of the night.

Because of Missy's baby, the Brave Women decided to postpone Estelle's shower until Missy could better deal with it emotionally. It was actually Estelle's idea. Everyone was surprised at her sudden considerateness, and no one was more so than Estelle herself.

Missy constantly assessed and wondered why her baby died. At first, she had entertained the notion that maybe if she were a different person, more...powerful, or something, that this wouldn't have happened. She believed that with some people, you could tell just by looking at them that nothing bad ever happened to them. Like all the popular cheerleaders in high school—it was a joke to think that any pain would ever get past those big smiles and high kicks. This philosophy had failed to provide her any comfort.

It was Kyle, at a Brave Women meeting, who pointed out that her vision was slightly flawed. "How do you know that cheerleaders don't feel pain?" she asked Missy. "In fact, how can you be sure about anyone's pain? You're being kind of presumptuous, aren't you, Missy?"

The others were very quiet. What was Kyle doing? Hadn't Missy been through enough?

Missy seemed eager to defend her bitter assessment. "You're telling me that you know someone who was one of those Ultra Brite cheerleaders in high school and she had pain in her life?"

"Yes," said Kyle. "As a matter of fact, I do. Me. I was one of those cheerleaders that you're so sure about."

"So was I," announced Diane.

"Me too," confessed Judy.

"I was a male cheerleader," said Allan.

"In my day, I was a cheerleader for the boys who were studying to be priests," said Estelle.

Missy would not budge. She addressed Kyle. "You don't look like you've had it too bad."

"You're right, Missy. It's a real treat to realize that when you and your lab partner are doing your chemistry homework, all you really want to do is bury your face in her breasts. That's definitely an easy thing to handle at sweet sixteen."

Missy acquiesced. At least she didn't have to deal with that. She was forced to acknowledge that a person could change, could overcome hardships and come out stronger for it.

Ever since that meeting, Missy had changed. She accepted her grief and took from it what she could. Soon, Todd noticed that when Estelle would walk into the same room that she was in, Missy didn't shrink and disappear, like she used to. It wasn't just Estelle, either, he said. Missy was acting different with just about everyone.

Missy noticed it, too. Since she had let the grief in, she felt different, on the whole. In fact, that was it, she told Todd. She felt more like a whole person. For the first time in her life she saw herself as solid, no longer a faint sketch of a quiet girl. It was as if this intense ache in her heart had…grounded her. Somehow she felt more centered, more connected to everything through the pain.

She decided to go for a solitary stroll.

It was a beautiful day and a relief just to get out. She walked a long time with no particular destination in mind. Missy looked up and found that she had wandered into the zoo. She spent the rest of the afternoon there, going in and out of the different animal houses. In the monkey house, a female had recently given birth to a baby monkey and one of the zoo keepers was giving it a bottle. Missy stood in front of the cage looking at the little monkey with diapers on, greedily sucking the milk from the bottle.

fifty seven

Allan had a bad feeling that since the hospital had failed before in their attempt to fire him, they were going to try to set him up. Perhaps they would pin one of their own malpractice mishaps on him, or even worse, create one for the sole purpose of getting rid of him. Everywhere Allan looked, people were backing off, not wanting to be seen with him. Obviously he had spoken up about patients' rights one time too many. He honestly thought he had the hospital over a barrel, what with all the things that they knew that he knew about. Radiology alone could keep him on the daytime talk show circuit for years, not to mention the hospital cafeteria.

No one wanted to take on the administration—not in this economy, anyway. Allan realized quickly that he was on his own, and if he were fired that no one was going to stick up for him. "If only there was a way I could open up my own hospital. I swear to God I would make sure patients received proper care instead of a bunch of screw-ups and padded bills." Allan held tight to his dream, and in the meantime watched Estelle very carefully. She was his friend and he certainly didn't want anything to happen to her or her baby.

Estelle's obstetrician was at the end of her rope. "Don't call me in the middle of the night any more with stupid questions," she griped. "I need my rest, too. After all, you're not the only one who's pregnant. I happen to be expecting also, so have some consideration, please."

"Oh, Doctor Gore, I had no idea," said Estelle.

"Well, now you know. Even though I'm a single woman with a history of failed relationships, I thought I'd make a fantastic parent. I just hope you don't go into labor in the morning—I have terrible morning sickness. Really, I don't know if I could stomach looking at a placenta in my condition. I hope your labor is fast—I'm not supposed to be on my feet for too long. I just pray to God that everything goes okay. It was the donor's last bit of sperm before he was suddenly killed in an explosion at NASA. But you look great. I'm sure everything is going to go smoothly with your delivery. The rest of us should be so lucky. Do you have a labor coach?"

"Yes, it's Allan Campbell."

"I know Allan." Dr. Gore rolled her eyes. She then checked her watch and exclaimed, "I've got to go, I've scheduled an ultrasound."

"I'm sorry," said Estelle. "I forgot, you do have other patients."

"It's for myself." And with that she was out the door of the examining room, leaving Estelle to wonder what kind of mother the doctor would be.

fifty eight

After taking four weeks to decide (Larry had begged Diane not to make a rash decision), Diane gave Larry the bad news that she was going back to Joe. She would, of course, have to quit the workshop. He simply asked her if she was sure, kissed her on the cheek, told her she had real talent, and made her promise to cultivate it. "And if you find that you made a mistake," he said, "I want you to call me, no matter how humiliated you might feel doing so. Please promise me."

"I will," she said, trying with all her might not to cry.

"I'm pretty sure I'll always love you," he said, and walked away.

His kindness touched Diane so much that when she thought of Joe she already doubted her decision. "Of course, maybe that's just a game Larry's playing. It's just a different kind of manipulation," she rationalized.

Estelle *was* swimming when her water broke, which is why she didn't realize it had happened. Instead, she and Missy got ready to go to another Brave Women meeting after Estelle returned from the pool. As they were walking out the front door, Todd stopped both of them and announced, "I have a surprise for you later on, Mom."

As they were all taking their seats in the W, Estelle couldn't stop herself from wondering what the surprise was. In fact it was more irritation than curiosity. "I'm in no mood for surprises—not with these damned false contractions." Estelle was convinced that she was in false labor because she was told as much by her obstetrician over the phone, who was too busy with her own pregnancy to take much notice. She decided to forget about the contractions as Diane called the meeting to order.

"For the first time," Diane began, "I'd like to ask the group's advice."

Everyone was quiet. They had never seen Diane like this. Gone was the protective designer armor. Instead they saw a vulnerable, thirty-nine-year-old woman, willing to reach out to people, to admit her own confusion. "For most of my life," she continued, "I've seen married men…" Diane paused. There was a disorientation about her tonight that was a little unsettling. She continued. "I'm seeing this man, but I can't stop thinking about this other man. Morning, noon and…"

Diane was interrupted by the faintest sound of crying. Not knowing who it was coming from, Diane searched all the faces until her eyes settled on the tiny, heaving shoulders of Judy, whose face was buried in her own hands. Diane turned to Kyle, who offered an immediate explanation.

"The artificial insemination didn't work again."

There were empathetic sighs accompanied by an extremely loud "OW!" Those who had merely sighed now looked for the source of the "OW!"

It had come from Estelle. She looked up and announced to the group, "Damn it to hell, I'm in labor! I knew it!"

Everyone was quiet. Nothing like this had ever come up at a meeting before. They stared at her. "What do we do?" they all wondered.

Privately deciding that Judy was in no shape to deliver a litter of puppies let alone a baby, Diane turned to Allan, who managed to stumble to his feet and declare that it would be all right.

"It's going to be all right. I'm a male nurse!"

The words didn't come as easily to him as they had in the past. He took a moment and closed his eyes and whispered an extremely brief prayer. Allan suddenly felt the enormity of the situation on his shoulders. He knew that they were all counting on him, it was only natural. "I can do this," he told himself.

He quickly took Estelle in his arms and gently guided her to the floor as the others slipped a cushion from the couch underneath her. Allan could see that Estelle was afraid. He was scared too, and hoped it didn't show. He needed to look like he was completely in control, for Estelle's sake. That was the first thing that you learned in nursing school: always try to instill as much confidence in the patient as you could. They took their confidence from you. Never show emotion.

"Should I call an ambulance?" asked Missy.

Allan didn't reply. He slipped on a stray latex glove from his coat pocket and did an internal. She was almost fully dilated. "I hate to say it, but it's a little too late for an ambulance," he announced. "Boil some water—we're going to have a baby!"

Though his hands were still shaking, Allan realized that he had been waiting for this his whole life. To be smack dab in the middle of a medical emergency where everyone else knew less than he did. He just prayed that he wouldn't mess up.

He was as prepared as he could have been. As Estelle's coach, he had been reading up on birthing babies.

"We can boil some water in my hot pot," said Diane, grateful now for something to do. "I hope he knows what he's doing," she thought. "Are you sure we need water? I always thought that was just an expression."

"It's not just an expression!" he shouted, sensing that

she was doubting him. He didn't need that. He needed support. After all, this was a support group, wasn't it? "We need the boiling water to sterilize towels and scissors for the baby."

"Oh," said the entire group.

"OW!" screamed Estelle.

"It's okay, I've done this a million times," said Allan. "In my mind," he said under his breath.

"I want a cigarette!" Estelle screamed. Missy was kneeling beside her, holding Estelle's hand.

"When I say push, then you push, okay?" asked Allan. "But not until I say to, otherwise you could tear yourself."

Estelle hated this. In her day the doctor would never speak to you. If he ever did, he always called her Mrs. Rogers. That's the way it should be, it was a sign of respect. She didn't want to know about things like tearing yourself. And for Gods sake, she didn't want all these women looking at her helshe area. Now everything was different. When she delivered her first two babies, there was no pain like this!

"HELL'S BELLS THIS HURTS!"

It was at that exact moment that Todd walked in with his surprise.

The voice made its way to Estelle through the pain. "Hello darlin'," it said. Estelle decided that she was dreaming. She thought she was hearing the voice of her husband. When the two men realized what was happening, each took a hand while Missy wiped Estelle's heavily powdered forehead.

"Push!" yelled Allan, which Estelle did obediently.

Kyle and Judy held hands.

"Please don't let anything happen to *this* baby," Missy secretly begged. Memories of her own delivery were sadly reawakened. Now she knew what it was like to have a life taken from you and she wouldn't wish that on anyone. Not even Estelle.

"Okay, Estelle, at the next contraction I want you to push again," said Allan. "Estelle! Estelle?" He was searching her face for some kind of sign as to how she was doing, but there was no response. Estelle was uncharacteristically silent. A shock wave went through the room.

"Oh my god," thought Missy, "she's having a stroke! She's way too old to be trying to give birth. Oh, please, God, let me be wrong."

She was. Estelle had simply gone to a place where women go during labor. A place where no man has ever gone, a place that Estelle didn't want to be. She could hear the voices but that was all. Unable to speak, she couldn't ask what she wanted to know: who the other voice belonged to, the familiar one with the southwestern twang. She thought it was just a side effect of labor.

The pain was overwhelming. "If only I could make my way to the letter opener on Diane's desk, then I could kill myself," she thought brightly. It was goals like these that kept Estelle going through the painful labor, which, she vowed to remember clearly while sitting on the witness stand in the lawsuit she planned on filing against the hospital for getting her pregnant.

The Brave Women were still scared out of their minds, for Estelle had never gone this long in a meeting without talking. Allan checked the vital signs of the mother and the baby. Finally, Estelle's face changed to the most hideous expression they had ever seen. These were the throes of death, they all thought. A mass feeling of guilt overcame them as each realized that he or she had fantasized about seeing this exact sight a hundred times. Estelle's expression worsened, which no one had thought possible. She lifted her head and her mouth opened. The group moved in to hear her. Were these to be her final words?

"I'll see those fertility doctors in their shallow graves!" she screamed at the exact moment that the baby made its way out of her body and into Allan's eager arms.

Everyone gasped, and then breathed a sigh of relief. This was the Estelle they knew. She was going to be all right. They applauded.

Allan quickly unblocked the infant's breathing passages with a Q-tip, checked the color of the skin, the reflexes, the eyes, and breathed a sigh of relief himself. The baby was perfectly healthy. Estelle lifted her head and saw that she had given birth to a beautiful little girl who was screaming her lungs out.

"She's Estelle's daughter all right," said Allan. The others nodded in agreement.

"Estelle," said Allan gently, "may I put your daughter on your chest?"

"I'll tell you what you can do," she replied. "You put that little dear on Missy's chest—if she's not wearing silk."

The others thought she was just delirious. Estelle was not delirious.

"Missy, lie down next to me…" Missy did as she was told. "…and let them put your daughter on your chest," screamed Estelle. Now everyone understood. Estelle *was* delirious…" Todd, Missy, I want you to raise this baby. She really belongs to you."

Missy did not hesitate or question. She simply held out her arms, the ones that had ached so much for a baby, and took the child.

In that instant, all of the doubt and confusion with which Diane had entered the meeting vanished. For the first time in her whole life she saw what she really wanted and knew that

Joe Della Femina could never give it to her.

In the same instant, Kyle and Judy each made up their minds to try artificial insemination as many times as they needed to. "Why not?" they said to each other. "I'd rather try and fail a thousand times if there's even a chance of having something like this..." They both looked on as Todd and Missy and their new baby got to know each other.

Todd Senior took Estelle's hand in his as she looked up at him and saw him for the first time in eighteen months. "I think I could live in Texas now," she said, slipping a Marlboro from the pack in his shirt pocket.

"I thought you said you didn't have the hair to live in Texas," he replied, fumbling for his lighter.

"Why do you think God invented wigs?" she asked as the first drag of smoke filled her tired lungs.

"Unless anyone else has anything to add, that's it for tonight's meeting. I'll see you all next week. I think that I speak for everyone when I say that, Estelle, you're all woman!" said Diane, for once allowing her tears to run freely down her cheeks.

fifty nine

Missy and Todd named their baby Daisy, because it was Missy's great grandmother's name and she had always liked it. Missy no longer doubted if she was strong enough to be a good parent. After all that had happened she knew that she could probably do anything. As Daisy filled their lives with love and laughter, Missy now encountered new feelings about Estelle. Although she was overwhelmed by Estelle's generosity, Missy now felt intense guilt whenever her mother-in-law irritated her. Consequently, she felt guilty all the time.

The good news was that Estelle was moving back to Texas with her husband, and with her, Missy hoped, would go the guilt. It was her own fault, she realized, giving in and paying credence to this form of self-loathing. That's what Todd said that Dr. Fellman said it was, allowing herself to feel guilt morning, noon and night was just a form of self-torture.

"Don't do this to yourself," begged her husband. "We need you, Daisy and I. I won't allow you to do this."

"I'm sorry," explained Missy. "I'm surprised at myself too. Just when I seem to have everything in the world: a beautiful little girl, a wonderful husband, Estelle moving across the country—now I start to feel really bad? It's frustrating beyond words."

Missy and Todd decided to drop it and get some sleep while they could, before the baby's next feeding.

Ever since the birth, Allan's confidence had soared. His job at St. Martina's now seemed to be holding him back, and he wondered if he should move on.

The experience had also altered his attitude toward women. He now had a healthier, more realistic view of them. It changed, he realized, in the moment that he thought Estelle might die. He had dealt with life and death before, but never with someone he knew. He had been unable to detach himself from the patient, as he had learned to do in nursing school, and as a result, he experienced something he never had before. He was forced to reconcile Estelle's strength with her complete helplessness. Allan observed a woman at her strongest and at her neediest, and found that he could accept both.

He recalled something that he had read once: I *am not a human being having a spiritual experience—I am a spiritual being having a human experience.* For the first time in his life, Allan saw the value of the human condition. He recognized the importance of imperfection.

He decided to reopen his relationship with his mother.

It was almost midnight on Sunday night. Diane stared at the letter she had just written to Joe. Earlier, she decided to write her feelings down, to sort them out, about how she didn't want to see him anymore and why. She then realized, after looking at what she had written, that this was the perfect way to dump the jerk. "Say it with Hallmark," she kept thinking, licking the envelope and putting a stamp marked LOVE on the upper right corner.

Having done that, Diane felt an unexpected wave of relief. "Strange," she thought to herself, "I feel like somewhere inside me something has...died? No," she decided, "that's not it. Something has definitely begun."

Her eyes traveled to the typewriter that she had set up on her dining room table months and months ago, when she stupidly vowed to write a book. "It's amazing how easy things seem to be after you have that second cup of coffee," she realized, disgusted and somewhat embarrassed with herself. She went over to the table, sat down, and immediately jumped up to apply a moisturizer. "No," she vowed, "Not this time." Diane then went back to the table and picked up one of Yelena's diaries. She started to read:

Dear Diary,

Today two men asked me to marry them! Oh diary, only in America could a commoner like me have two men fighting for my callused hand in marriage. You know them both, diary. One is the rich owner of the fish factory where I work. He said that if I marry him my hours will be better. I won't have to work the fourteen hour shift anymore—I'll be allowed to take the ten hour one instead so that I could be home to cook his suppers. Just imagine, diary: me, plain old Yelena Helgit, a lady of leisure!

The other man is also one you know, Slak Yorvik. It's strange, but in Kebashnik, Slak was royalty and I was a Plotz. And here in America, Slak Yorvik is no longer royalty, he's just another immigrant looking for work. It's funny how now that I see Slak in America I don't love him like I did in Kebashnik. Why?

I can't help but smile when I think that a rich man wants to marry me...I

think that tomorrow, after I finish
pricing all the fish heads, I will say
yes to marriage. The man that I choose
will be my boss because he is more like
America to me. I am sorry, Slak.

Diane thought about Larry.

sixty

"Come in, please," offered Dr. Fellman, indicating the patient chair to Missy.

"Thank you."

Silence.

"Have you ever been in therapy before?"

Dr. Fellman was a little surprised by the question.

"Uh, I…well, yes," she was relieved to be able to answer. "Yes, I've been in therapy. How about you?"

"No."

"Would you like to be?" asked Dr. Fellman.

"So far, no," she answered. "If this is what it's like."

"Well, usually there's a little more to it than this, believe me. But it's up to you. It's absolutely something you shouldn't do unless you want to."

"That sounds rehearsed," said Missy, "But in a way it's refreshing."

"How so?" asked the doctor.

"Well, you make it sound so enticing by insisting that I shouldn't do therapy unless I really want to. I didn't expect that. I thought that I would come in here and you would tell me how much I need your help."

Dr. Fellman smiled. "I'm not sure you do."

"What?"

"I'm not sure you need my help. You sound like you're doing pretty well on your own."

"So why am I here?"

"What a great question."

Silence.

"Well," said Missy, "I don't know if you know anything about Todd's mother…"

"Believe me, I know everything about Todd's mother. And then some," said Dr. Fellman.

"Oh. Well maybe this won't take as long as I thought. See, my mother-in-law...I had her pegged in my mind..."

"In what way did you have her 'pegged'?"

"I thought Todd told you all about Estelle," said Missy.

"Of course he did. But that's Todd's perception of her, which won't do *us* much good. I'm interested in how *you* see Estelle, in how *you've* pegged her, to use your expression."

"Mean."

"Really?"

Missy was taken aback, "Yes. Why, do you doubt me?"

"It's not that I doubt you," explained Dr. Fellman, "But if you really just thought of Estelle as mean, you wouldn't have a problem."

"Why not?"

"If you really knew she was mean, you wouldn't have a conflict with her. For example, if you know someone is truly insane, you just accept it, you don't get mad at them, because you know they're insane and you write it off. They're insane—no doubt about it, no problem. Sounds like you doubt how you've pegged her."

"So if I really thought she was mean, it wouldn't bother me much?" asked Missy.

"Exactly. There is a conflict; the conflict is with you. Estelle reflects a struggle going on inside you."

"Okay," said Missy, "It's my fault. Everything is..."

Just then Missy opened her eyes and saw Todd sitting up beside her in bed. "Oh, I had the weirdest dream. I dreamed..."

"I know all about it. I was there, sort of," explained Todd.

"What do you mean, you were there?"

"You were talking in your sleep, I heard you, so I started answering your questions like I thought Dr. Fellman would," said Todd.

"All those insightful things came from you?"

He nodded.

"I don't know what to say. You should be a therapist."

"I'm pretty impressed myself," admitted Todd, smiling.

sixty one

It was Sunday night, about ten o'clock. Diane was just returning from a Brave Women meeting. She was happy because Judy and Kyle had finally gotten pregnant—both of them (they each decided to go through the procedure to double their chances). The Brave Women were all *so* happy for them. In a way, though, it made one Brave Woman feel lonelier than ever. "Maybe it's just because it's Sunday night," she thought.

When Diane got to her door, there was an envelope on the floor in front of it. Curious, she took it inside and opened it. Inside was a magazine—*GQ*. The magazine fell open to a specific page where Diane noticed a lime green Post-It Note. Her eyes were drawn to the title of the article that began there: *The Privilege Was Mine*, by Larry York. Stunned, she glanced at the story briefly and then skipped to the last paragraph.

> Sometimes, in the middle of the night, I wake up and remember that we were lovers once, but that it's over. I don't cry, however, because I am too busy laughing at myself for even thinking that you could ever be mine. I suppose it's just human nature to dare to dream, to wonder why everyone else is so lucky and not you.
>
> I have not one regret, Diane, for to have known you is to have known all that is divinely female. You filled my senses with your life-spirit, and touched my hand with your soul. I will never forget you for teaching me the true meaning of love and for showing me the real beauty of a woman.